murder in the maze

MURDER IN THE MAZE

LLOYD BIGGLE, JR.

A
GRANDFATHER RASTIN
MYSTERY NOVEL

TRANSCRIBED BY
KENNETH LLOYD BIGGLE

WILDSIDE PRESS

The locale of this novel (fictitious Borg County, Michigan) and several of the main characters have been developed in a series of short stories, published primarily in *Ellery Queen's Mystery Magazine* and also republished in the short story collection, *The Grandfather Rastin Mysteries*.

Published by Wildside Press, LLC.
www.wildsidepress.com

CHAPTER 1

In the first place, my Grandfather Rastin never should have bought that house in Wiston. It happened several years ago, when he was only about seventy-eight, but even so he was old enough to know better. He admits that himself.

In the second place, he should have asked his tenants for references.

He did buy the house, and he didn't ask for references, and that's why, on a lovely June afternoon, I was driving him to Wiston instead of going swimming at Hodges' Quarry as I'd planned. The tenants hadn't paid their rent, and they didn't answer the telephone, and Grandfather wanted to find out what was going on.

It was just about two o'clock when we reached the long level stretch of Highway 29 midway between Borgville and Wiston. On one side of the road was what some farmer hoped would eventually be a field of corn. On the other side was a tall hedge which a number of people claim is three hundred feet long, though I have never heard of anyone taking the trouble to measure it. In the whole stretch of hedge there was just one opening, and beside the opening, facing in both directions, were signs that read, "SALESMEN WELCOME."

That afternoon there were two cars parked beside the signs. Grandfather nudged me as we approached, and I steered my jalopy off the road and stopped. Grandfather got out and I opened all four doors to get some fresh air into the car. It was a hot afternoon but Grandfather always insists on keeping car windows closed, regardless of the temperature. This attitude of his dates back to the winter of 1925, when he claims he lost his hair from riding around in an open car. I've pointed out many times that he hasn't any more hair to lose, and anyway, an open car in the winter and an open window in the summer are not the same thing, but when you argue with Grandfather all you get out of it is exercise for your jaw muscles.

I was glad enough to stop and get the car cooled off, and Grandfather went over to talk with Ed Fellows who was sitting in one of the parked cars.

"Ed saw a salesman go through the hedge," Grandfather said, when he came back. "That's his car."

"How long ago?" I asked.

"Maybe ten, fifteen minutes. Shall we wait?"

"Suit yourself," I said. "I won't get home in time to go swimming anyway."

Grandfather went back to talk with Ed and I got a paper-back mystery out of the glove compartment and settled down to read.

A little later Sam Baker happened along and he stopped, and then came Mr. Crabtree, who is the janitor for the Borgville First Baptist Church, and Ed Carter, who has a farm the other side of Borgville, and three or four others, and that stretch of Highway 29 began to look like the overflow from a farm auction.

We'd been there for the best part of an hour when Steve Carling came by. Steve is a deputy sheriff, though not the smartest one even in Borg County, but when he saw that many cars stopped along the road he got the idea right away that someone might be wanting the law. He gave his siren a couple of blasts and edged the patrol car in behind my jalopy.

"What's up?" he asked.

"Nothing much," I said. "Just waiting for a salesman to come out."

"You're kidding," Steve said. "You mean there was one who hasn't heard about this place?"

"This is a main highway," I said. "The professor's bound to catch a stranger now and then. This one has an Ohio license plate."

"Well, he'll be looking for a cop when he comes out, so I suppose I might as well wait." Steve likes to call himself a cop, though as far as I know no one else does, and Grandfather says it's about what you can expect when you let the uneducated masses watch television. Steve called Sheriff Pilkins on the radio, and got the sheriff's okay, and then he went over to join the crowd around Ed Fellows' car.

By this time we were all getting impatient, and though it was still the middle of the afternoon Ed Fellows began to worry about getting home by milking time. "Nothing ties a man down more than a herd of cows," Ed said, and Sam Baker, who has nine children, told Ed he didn't know what he was talking about.

There were two schools of thought on this particular salesman. One held that he was dumber than most salesmen, and wouldn't be seen again until a rescue expedition went after him. The other held that he was smarter than most salesmen, and it was taking longer to come out because he'd gone in further. It was a pretty futile subject for an argument, since Ed Fellows was the only one of them that had seen the man and he hadn't had more than a glimpse of his back, but I guess arguing is as good a way as any to pass the time.

Finally Grandfather said to Steve Carling, "Give us a couple more hoots on your siren. That might hurry him up."

"Naw," Steve said. "Once he starts back he won't need nothing to hurry him."

But Steve started over to his car to use the siren, and then he stopped by the hedge and said, "I think he's coming."

Someone was coming. We could hear the footsteps on the gravel paths, so all of us lined up by the opening in the hedge, and waited. There was one final rush, with a little skidding as the salesman turned a corner, and then he popped out through a break in the hedge and pulled up to stare at us.

He was a youngish-looking fellow, and also good-looking, but he'd lost his slicked-up salesman look somewhere on the other side of the hedge. His hair was mussed up, and sweat was dripping from his face and had soaked right through his suit coat around his arms and back. He still had his briefcase, though, and if he was fagged out and breathing heavily, at least he wasn't scared. I've seen salesmen come out of there so scared they couldn't talk. This one looked us over, and then spotted Steve Carling, who was in uniform.

He walked up to Steve, and said, "Officer, there's a dead man in there."

That was when we started to laugh.

Ed Fellows doubled up, holding his stomach. Mr. Carter threw his head back and cackled like a turkey. The others all had their own individual styles, even Grandfather, who usually chuckles without making any noise. The total uproar was considerable, and through it all the salesman stood there with his mouth open, probably convinced that he'd happened onto a crowd of raving idiots.

When the laughter had quieted down to just a straggling snicker or two, Steve Carling slapped the salesman on the back and told him there wasn't anything to worry about.

"That place you were in," he said. "It belongs to one of those college professors. He's a—a—"

"Psychologist," Grandfather said.

"Sure," Steve said. "One of those. And the thing you've been wandering around in, that's called a—a—"

"Maze," Grandfather said.

"Sure. Maze. This Professor Pesman, he's got some notion that rats are smarter than people, so he built this maze thing, and up at the house he has a model of it. He likes to time how long it takes a person to find his way out of it, and then he puts a rat in the one up at the house, and times the rat, and then he writes a book about how much smarter the rat is."

"Very interesting," the salesman said. "But there's *still* a dead man in there, though I'll have a hard time showing you exactly where."

"Well, now, it's like this," Steve said. "People hereabouts got tired a long time ago of being compared with rats, and the professor had trouble finding anyone who'd run around in this maze for him, even if he paid them. So he put up these 'SALESMEN WELCOME' signs, and he had an electric eye thing installed in the hedge to ring a bell up at the house when-ever a sucker accepts the invitation. And all around the maze he's scattered dummies. They're laid out to look like dead people, and whatever way you go, you're sure to see one sooner or later. The professor wants the suckers to try to get out of there as fast as they can, and he figures there's nothing that will hurry a man quite as much as falling over a dead body. When he hears the bell, he takes a spyglass and a stop watch and goes up to a little dome on top of the house, and as soon as the sucker finds a dummy and starts running the professor times him."

The salesman got out his handkerchief, and mopped his face. If he was feeling doggone mad about the whole business, as he should have been, he didn't let it show much. "It was a very realistic dummy," he said.

"I've never seen one myself," Steve said. "But I've heard they're darned realistic. They're supposed to have bashed heads, and knives stick-ing in them, and all kinds of stuff like that. They tell me the old boy even pours ketchup on them."

"This one had ketchup," the salesman said. He mopped his face again. "Well, I guess I'll be going."

Steve pounded his back. "Don't take it so hard. You aren't the first, by a long way. And if I were you I'd give it another try and see if I could find my way up to the house. The professor has a standing guarantee that if any salesman gets through to the house he'll buy six of whatever he's selling."

"You know," the salesman said, "I'm just disgusted enough to give it another try. I'd enjoy telling this professor what I think of him."

And he turned around and zipped back through the hedge before the rest of us could stop him.

"You shouldn't have done that," Grandfather said.

"It won't cost him any more than a little time," Steve said. "And he looks like a smart fellow. Maybe he'll make it."

"No one ever has yet," Grandfather said. "The professor's probably in his laboratory right now, checking this guy's time with one of his rats, and he might be too interested to hear the bell. You'd better telephone the house, and tell them, so this salesman won't end up spending the night in the maze."

"Well, it won't be any trouble to do that," Steve said.

The meeting broke up, and Grandfather and I went to Wiston. A few miles up the road Grandfather scratched his head, and said, "You know, I've seen that salesman around here before."

"I suppose that's possible," I said. "Salesmen have territories, and may-be his is Borg County."

"He wasn't carrying a briefcase the last time I saw him," Grandfather said. "He was—"

He went on muttering to himself.

A couple of miles further on, he said, "I wonder what he was selling."

"You should have asked him when you had a chance," I said. "By this time he may be lost in the maze permanently."

Grandfather didn't answer, but he was doing a powerful lot of thinking. So much, in fact, that he didn't notice I had my window down until we were almost to Wiston.

CHAPTER II

Professor Charles Pesman came to Borg County, Michigan, in 1935. He bought the Courthouse, and built a maze, and these two things would probably be the leading tourist attractions of Borg County, if it wasn't for the fact that Borg County doesn't have any tourists.

I should explain that the Courthouse is not the official county courthouse, but one that was built back in the 1840's by a fussy old geezer named Ebenezer Borg. The official county courthouse is in Wiston, which naturally is the county seat, and most people refer to it as the County Building. As far as I know, that one has never been for sale.

Old Ebenezer wanted the Borg County seat located between Borgville and Wiston, where he had a big farm that he claimed was the geographical center of the county. He laid out a town there, and to cinch matters he even built a courthouse, figuring he could sell it to the county later.

Unfortunately for him, no one wanted to live in his town. Wiston became the county seat, a county building was built there, and Ebenezer was left with one surplus courthouse. Not being the kind of person who lets things go to waste, he moved into it himself and lived there the rest of his life. And since he was a stubborn man, he never called his house anything but the Courthouse. The people in Borg County go along with a gag about as well as people anywhere, and Ebenezer's white elephant has been the Courthouse ever since.

The old place was really run-down by the time Professor Pesman bought it. He spent a lot of money landscaping it and fixing it up. Then, between the Courthouse and the highway, he put up the darndest pattern of woven wire fences anyone ever saw anywhere. He planted a special kind of hedge on each side of the fences, and when the hedges grew up he had his maze.

The hedges are seven feet high now, and there's no telling how high they'd be if they weren't trimmed regularly. What with that tall hedge along the highway, and a big grove of trees on each side, a tourist couldn't even see the Courthouse except from a side road.

It didn't take Professor Pesman long to establish himself as a rare kind of character, even in Borg County where we have more than our share of characters. Some people thought he had an unusual sense of humor, but they were mostly people who had never known him personally. He spent a lot of time working on elaborate gags, such as chairs wired to give a pretty stiff electric shock, and soda pop with laxative in it, and pretty bouquets of flowers of which the principal ingredient was poison ivy. The professor never called these things jokes, which is just as well, because I never saw anyone on the receiving end who thought they were funny. They were *scientific* experiments. The professor always pronounced the word that way—*sci*entific. He made it sound like something a decent man wouldn't do to his worst enemy, and often enough it was. Those "SALESMEN WELCOME" signs out by the highway were another of his *sci*entific experiments.

I'd had some experience in that maze myself, and I felt sorry for any man foolish enough to tackle the thing twice on one afternoon. I wanted Grandfather to call the professor himself, when we got to Wiston, but we found enough problems there to make us forget all about the salesman.

Grandfather's tenants had moved out without telling him, breaking their lease, and they left the house a mess. I went to work cleaning up the place while Grandfather bustled around trying to trace the tenants. He was in a particularly nasty mood because the tenant's deposit probably wouldn't cover the damage done to the house, and when we finally took the time to go to a restaurant for supper he was almost too mad to eat.

"I never should have bought a house in Wiston in the first place," he said. "Nothing good ever happens in this town."

"Why don't you sell it?" I asked.

"Sell it? In the condition it's in, I couldn't even give it away!"

It was dark when we finally left Wiston. We were both in a hurry to get home, so I put the accelerator on the floor. I had my jalopy doing forty-five when we reached the level stretch by the Courthouse, and that's as fast as it'll go anywhere except downhill. As we were passing the maze Grandfather grabbed my arm and yelled, "Stop!"

I pulled off the road and stopped. "What's the matter?" I asked.

"Wasn't that the salesman's car parked back there?"

I'd been concentrating so much on getting home that I hadn't even seen a car. I made a U-turn and drove back, and there it was, parked right by the opening into the maze.

"Isn't that his car?" Grandfather asked.

"I didn't pay much attention this afternoon," I said. "But it's parked right where his was parked, and it has Ohio license plates."

"I'll bet that idiot Steve Carling didn't telephone the house, and he's been lost in there all afternoon."

Grandfather got out of the car, and hollered, "Hey, there!"

From somewhere off in the maze a male voice answered. It said, "Help!"

"All right," Grandfather shouted back. "You'll get help."

He got back into the car, and I drove around to the entrance to the Courthouse.

This took considerably longer that it takes to tell about it. The Courthouse is located between U.S. 29 and Sandpiper Road, which angles in to intersect the highway a couple of miles to the north. We had to drive down to the intersection, and then go back on Sandpiper Road to the private drive that leads down to the Courthouse. The maze is only on the highway side, but there's a hedge all around the grounds, and a steel gate where the drive comes in, and to my disgust and Grandfather's astonishment the gate was shut and padlocked.

I honked my horn, and turned my lights on and off, and Grandfather got out of the car and shouted, but for a long time—twenty minutes, anyway—nothing happened. Then outside lights came on all over the place, and a little later we saw Nat Barlow hobbling down the drive towards the gate.

Nat's an old timer who's been a friend of Grandfather's for at least sixty years, but there are very few places I would have expected to find him at that time of night, and the Courthouse wasn't one of them.

"What's Nat doing here?" I asked.

"The professor gave him a job," Grandfather said.

"Doing what?"

"When I talked to Nat, he didn't know exactly what he was supposed to do."

"He probably still doesn't know," I said.

Grandfather was all set to blast Nat good for taking so long, but he never got around to it. Before Nat got to the gate a car drove up behind mine, and Sheriff Pilkins got out.

As soon as the sheriff saw Grandfather he used some language that is not proper for an elected servant of the people, and I'm sure that Grandfather reciprocated in kind, only Grandfather kept his under his breath.

"Who gave you permission to be out this late?" the sheriff said. And Grandfather came right back, "Gadding around again at the taxpayers' expense, aren't you?" And then they really started it.

The fact is that Grandfather and the sheriff don't like each other. This is only partly because the sheriff is a Republican—you have to be, to get elected to anything in Borg County—and Grandfather is the only Democrat in Borgville who admits it. They don't agree about anything else, either, but they argue a little louder when the subject is politics. At this time they were still having a difference of opinion about the election that happened in the fall of 1962.

In that election Borgville cast twenty-three votes against Sheriff Pilkins, leaving him with a victory margin of only about fifteen to one. The sheriff did a little arithmetic, and decided that his opponent's relatives couldn't account for more than eleven of the votes, and Grandfather's vote only made twelve, so someone must have stuffed the ballot box. He didn't come right out and accuse Grandfather, but he hinted.

While they were arguing Nat finally got the gate open, and I interrupted to point out to Grandfather that we had business to attend to if the salesman hadn't already died of exposure.

"What are you doing here, anyway?" Grandfather asked the sheriff.

"Mrs. Glover called, and said gangsters were trying to break the gate down," the sheriff said. "What's your excuse?"

That started them off again, since Grandfather had to tell the sheriff what an idiot Steve Carling was for sending the salesman back into the maze and not telling the professor about it, and the sheriff said if it were time to pass out awards for idiocy Grandfather could move to the head of the line, because Steve had telephoned, and he, the sheriff, had been in the office at the time and heard him.

Finally I went back to the house with Nat, and left the two of them arguing.

Mrs. Glover was waiting at the door with a rifle in her hands. It was a Civil War rifle, and if it could have been fired it probably would have been about equally dangerous at either end. The professor's grandfather or uncle or somebody had brought it home from the war, and the professor kept it hanging on the wall in the big dining room.

"Oh, it's you, Johnny," Mrs. Glover said. "Why in the world did you have to scare us to death?"

"What do you mean, scare you to death?" I asked.

"Why, lights flashing on and off, and all that noise, and then the maze bell started ringing, and I thought we were being attacked."

The bell was still ringing. It was located in the hallway between the kitchen and the living room, and it didn't make a lot of noise but it kept giving out a bong every now and then. That was weird, because usually it just rang once, when someone walked through the opening out by the highway.

"I don't know about the bell," I said, "but someone's lost in the maze, and we wanted to tell you so the guy wouldn't have to spend the night there. And the gate was locked."

She clucked her tongue, and tut-tutted a few times, and said something would have to be done about that, and Nat stood looking on with a contented smile on his face. Nat's a nice fellow, in his seventies, and a great friend of Grandfather's and for as long as I could remember he'd been skinny and irritable and a regular fuss-budget. After only a week at the Courthouse he'd already put on weight and started to look domesticated.

Mrs. Glover was responsible for that. She was a good-looking woman with a lot of talent for making a man feel contented. I thought she talked too much, but she also was a real good cook, and I guess a man doesn't mind listening to a woman talk if he can eat while she does it. Anyway, the men at the Courthouse all tended to be on the plump side, except for Willie, who didn't count anyway, and any stranger who entered the place faced a double danger, because if the professor didn't make a guinea pig out of him, there was Mrs. Glover in the kitchen waiting to fatten him up. She had a habit of poking me in the ribs with her thumb, and then she'd cluck her tongue a couple of times and bring out a piece of pie and a glass of milk. I liked to eat as well as the next person, but I get self-conscious about it when some-one feels my ribs before and afterwards.

Grandfather and the sheriff came in, and Mrs. Glover sent Nat after Mr. Boyd, who was the professor's assistant. The bell kept on ringing. Mr. Boyd came down a little later, wearing a contented look like everyone else in the place, though he needed a shave and there was a faint aroma about him that did not originate in any perfume bottle. It very strongly reminded me of Bailey's Bar.

He was wearing pajamas and an old robe, though it did not seem to be anyone's bedtime at the Courthouse, and when Grandfather told him about the man in the maze he came up with a few choice expressions of his own, despite the fact that there was a lady present.

"I wanted the prof to put a gate out there," he said. "But he wouldn't do it. Well, I'm not going after the guy. Get Willie."

"I'll get him," I said.

I went down to Willie's basement room and knocked a couple of times on the door, and then I opened it. I didn't wait for an invitation because Willie was dumb—not the stupid kind of dumb, but the kind that can't talk. Around the Courthouse he was sometimes referred to as Silly-Willie, but I thought he had as much brains as anyone else there, and maybe just a little more. I'd noticed that he knew the professor's maze backwards and there was nothing silly about his technique when he played checkers. It was positively devastating.

Willie was sitting on his bed reading one of the professor's psychology books. At least he was looking at it. No one knew whether he could read or not, on account of his never saying anything.

"Knock it off, Willie," I said. "Someone's lost in the maze."

He nodded, and put the book down, and went loping off in that funny way he had, with his head stuck out in front of him and squinting through his glasses. Mr. Boyd once told me there wasn't anything in the glasses but window glass and I thought maybe that was why Willie squinted. I had to admit that he usually looked pretty silly, always needing a haircut, and wearing baggy old clothes that looked big enough to hold two of him, and with his squint and his funny way of walking, but he certainly didn't act silly.

I went back upstairs. Mr. Boyd was saying, "Sure—Steve called. Must have been around three-thirty. I went right out to do my good deed for the day, but if anyone was in the maze he didn't answer when I called, and there wasn't any car parked out by the highway, so I figured he found his way out the way he came in, and left."

"There," the sheriff said. "You owe Steve an apology."

"His remembering to make one phone call doesn't make him any the less an idiot," Grandfather said. "I could cite a few other instances—"

"Can it!" Sheriff Pilkins yelled. "I never claimed he was the brains of my department."

"Since when have there been any brains in your department?" Grandfather asked.

That would have started them off again if Mr. Boyd hadn't interrupted. "What's this about Steve sending the guy back in?" he asked. "All he told me was that someone had gone into the maze, and I should check before dark to see if he was still there."

"Isn't someone going to do something about that bell?" Mrs. Glover asked.

"Willie's gone to see about it," Mr. Boyd said. "Now, about Steve sending this guy back in—"

Grandfather told him about the convention we'd held, waiting for the salesman to come out, and how Steve had told him about the professor's guarantee, and he'd gone back into the maze to try and collect it.

"It sounds fishy to me," Mr. Boyd said. "You say he found one of the dummies?"

"Found it and came tearing out of there," Grandfather said.

"That's real odd," Mr. Boyd said. "Because there aren't any dummies out there."

Grandfather arched his eyebrows, and the sheriff sat looking at Mr. Boyd with a blank expression on his face. Just then Willie came in leading a stranger. He was a dried-up looking little fellow, at least fifty years old and maybe older, and though he was dressed in one of these fancy summer suits he looked as if he'd been through a war.

"How long have you been out there?" Mr. Boyd asked.

"Since about four o'clock," he said. He sounded hoarse, probably from shouting for help.

Mrs. Glover came in from the kitchen to remind us that the bell was still ringing. "See what it is," Mr. Boyd told Willie, and Willie nodded and went out again.

"Is this the guy?" the sheriff asked Grandfather.

Grandfather shook his head. "The one we saw was a young fellow."

"If he's been out there since four, he's probably hungry," Mr. Boyd said. "Ruth—feed the man. He hasn't had supper."

"Why, you poor man!" Mrs. Glover said. She didn't exactly prod him in the ribs, but she did pat his arm, and he followed her out to the kitchen.

"Where's the professor?" Grandfather wanted to know.

"Up in the lab, doing some kind of special experiment," Mr. Boyd said.

"Get him down here," the sheriff said. "That maze of his is getting to be a public nuisance. If he doesn't put up a gate, and take down those signs, I'm going to ask the county attorney to get a court order."

"Tell him some other time," Mr. Boyd said. "He chased everyone out and he said he didn't want to be interrupted until he'd finished."

"There isn't any light in the laboratory," Grandfather said.

"You can't see his desk light from the outside. Did this salesman say he found a dummy?"

"No," Grandfather said. "He said he found a dead man."

The sheriff half got to his feet and then sat down again. "I don't like this," he announced.

"Are you sure there aren't any dummies out there?" Grandfather asked.

"Positive," Mr. Boyd said. "I brought them in myself. All twelve of them. They were in pretty sad shape, from lying out there in the weather. They'll have to be renovated."

"Maybe the professor put one of them back. Or maybe Willie did."

"I doubt it," Mr. Boyd said. "You can ask Willie when he comes back."

"Supposing you check now," the sheriff said, "and see if one of them is missing."

Mr. Boyd shook his head. "They're up in the lab, and when the prof says he doesn't want to be bothered, he doesn't want to be bothered."

"He's going to be bothered," the sheriff said. "Right now."

Mr. Boyd grinned, and shook his head again. "I like my job here."

The sheriff glared, and Mr. Boyd, still looking contented, took his time about lighting a cigarette. We sat there waiting for Willie.

He came in a few minutes later, with Ed Fellows. He looked surprised to see the sheriff. He said, "Did you find the guy?"

"Mr. Rastin drove around to tell us," Mr. Boyd said. "But thanks anyway."

"That's okay," Ed said. "I saw the car, and I wanted you to know, so I've been walking back and forth through the hedge to make the bell ring. If Willie will take me back, I'll be on my way."

"Just a moment," Sheriff Pilkins said. "Were you here this afternoon when that salesman was in the maze?"

"Sure," Ed said. "I was the one that saw him go in."

"Did you see him come out?"

"Sure. I was the first one to stop, and I waited. He was an awful long time about it."

"What was it he said when he came out?"

"He said there was a dead man in there—just like they usually do, you know. I've seen a lot of them. I always wait when there's a car parked there."

"Do you still say all the dummies are up in the lab?" the sheriff asked Mr. Boyd.

"All of *our* dummies are up in the lab," he said. "Unless—Willie, did you put one of the dummies back in the maze?"

Willie said "Un," which was the extent of his vocabulary, and shook his head.

"Did the prof?"

Willie shook his head again.

"Then how do you account for that salesman finding a dummy?" the sheriff asked.

"I don't," Mr. Boyd said. "Unless he brought his own."

"Either the guy was lying, or—"

Grandfather interrupted. "He wasn't lying."

"I don't like this one bit. Before I go home tonight, I aim to find out just what happened out there. Right now I want those dummies in the laboratory counted."

"You won't get it done by me," Mr. Boyd said.

The sheriff turned to Willie. "Willie, I'm the sheriff of Borg County, and I need your cooperation. Will you go up to the laboratory and count the dummies?"

Willie looked at Mr. Boyd. Then he shook his head.

"He likes his job, too," Mr. Boyd said.

The sheriff's face is the most expressive thing about him, especially when he's mad. That time it registered several shades of deepening pink on its way to becoming a violent red. I watched him with real interest, because I've never seen it go beyond purple, and I've always wondered what the next color would be. Red was as far as it went, though. Mrs. Glover had been listening from the kitchen door and she came in and wanted to know what the fuss was about.

"What a bunch of dummies you are," she said, "getting all worked up over a bunch of dummies. I'll count them myself."

And she did. She went up to the laboratory, which was the whole third floor of the Courthouse, and she counted the dummies. Then she came down and told us she'd counted twelve, so they were all there.

"What'd the prof say?" Mr. Boyd asked.

"Nothing," she said. "He wasn't there."

"Oh," Mr. Boyd said. "Then the experiment didn't work out, and he went to bed peeved."

"Without any supper," Mrs. Glover said.

"Does that happen often?" the sheriff asked.

"Not often," Mrs. Glover said. "But it happens."

"Well, get him out of bed," the sheriff said. "It's time we heard what he has to say about this."

Mr. Boyd shrugged his shoulders. "Like I said, I like my job."

"Phooey!" Mrs. Glover said. "It isn't your job that worries you—you're just too lazy to move. I'll get him up."

"By all means," Mr. Boyd said. "You do it. He never minds when *you* wake him up."

Mrs. Glover hissed something at him, and then she went up the big curving staircase. What Mr. Boyd said must have irked her, because going up the staircase she flounced, if that word means what I think it does. There was nothing fancy about the way she came down, except it was fast.

"He isn't there," she said.

No one said anything for a long time. The sheriff was looking at Grandfather, and Grandfather was very slowly nodding his head.

"When did you see the professor last?" the sheriff asked.

"Right after lunch," Mr. Boyd said. "Jerry Krohl was out to talk to him about some investments, and after Jerry left he told me he was going to work on a special experiment and he didn't want to be bothered until he finished. Period."

"You haven't seen him since?"

Mr. Boyd shook his head.

"How about you?" the sheriff asked Mrs. Glover.

"I haven't seen him since lunch," she said. "I saw Mr. Krohl when he left, but I didn't see the professor then."

"What time was that?"

"It couldn't have been long after twelve-thirty. We had an early lunch today."

The sheriff turned to Willie. "Have you seen the professor since lunch?"

Willie said "Uh," and shook his head.

"How about you, Nat?"

"Haven't seen him since lunch," Nat said. "I helped Pete trim trees all afternoon."

"Where's Pete?"

"In his room."

Willie went after Pete Kruger. He'd fallen asleep with his clothes on, and he came downstairs rubbing his eyes and stood blinking at the sheriff. Pete was a quaint old guy. With his white hair and wrinkled face he looked years older than Nat Barlow, though I don't think he was over sixty. One of his jobs was looking after the professor's laboratory animals, and he took care of them so well that by comparison every child in Borg County was being neglected. Where people were concerned he wasn't so gentle. He had a terrible temper, and it was fascinating to listen to him swear because he never used swear words. He said a preacher had once told him that if he had to be profane he could do it with words that wouldn't offend the Lord, so he'd made up his own swear words. They sounded like nothing I ever heard before, but when he used them there wasn't any doubt about what he meant.

He was still half asleep, and for a moment the sheriff's questions didn't register. "Ain't seen the professor since lunch," he said, when he finally understood.

A white mouse came out of Pete's overall pocket, ran up across his shoulders, and disappeared into a pocket on the other side. The sheriff rubbed his eyes. "Where's the telephone?" he asked.

He went into the kitchen to make a telephone call. When he came back, he pointed to Willie. "I want you to get out by the road and stand in that gap in the hedge. Don't let anyone in—or out. If anyone tries to get by, scream."

"Now how would he do that?" Mr. Boyd asked.

The sheriff considered this, and changed his plan. "Take Nat out there," he said to Willie. "You know what to do, Nat. And Willie, you come right back here. I have more important things for you to do, anyway. I've got four men coming, and when they get here—by the way, what happened to that salesman you were feeding?"

"He's still in the kitchen eating," Mrs. Glover said.

"He wasn't in there just now."

Mrs. Glover headed for the kitchen, with the sheriff right behind her. It was a tossup as to which of them was the maddest.

"The idea!" Mrs. Glover said, waving her arms. "He ate two ham sandwiches and a piece of chocolate cake, and he left without saying thank you. He didn't even finish his coffee."

"He probably went out the back way, and circled around the outside of the maze," the sheriff said. "You say his car was parked out by the highway?"

"It was when I came in," Ed Fellows said.

"You go along with Nat and Willie. If the car's still there, you stay and make sure he doesn't get away in it. If it's gone, come back with Willie, and tell me.

The three of them went out.

"When my men get here," the sheriff said, "I want to go over that maze inch by inch. I want to find this dummy that scared the salesman."

Mr. Boyd stared at him. "Are you crazy? Do you know how many inches there are in that maze? It's three hundred feet square, and there aren't any lights out there. We'll be a week flushing deputy sheriffs out of it."

"We'll put lights out there," the sheriff said. "And don't you worry about my deputies getting lost. They can holler as loud as any salesman."

A little time later Ed came back with Willie, and said that the salesman's car was gone. Right away the sheriff wanted to know what kind of car it was and what license number it had. Ed and I couldn't agree on either the year or the make, and neither of us had noticed the license, except it was from Ohio. The sheriff waved his arms is disgust.

Grandfather sent me to telephone Mom. "Tell her," he said, "that if things work out the way I expect, we may not be home at all tonight." I told her, and then the deputies came, and we all moved out to the maze.

We probably would have been there all night if Mr. Boyd hadn't had a bright idea right from the start. "The salesman went in at the other end," he said, "so let's work from there. He might have gotten himself into an alley we can't even reach from this side."

So we went around to the entrance by the highway, and it turned out that Sheriff Pilkins and his deputies were surplus baggage as far as exploring mazes was concerned. Mr. Boyd brought out a map of the thing, and he and Willie worked together, Willie exploring all the alleys and turns and lanes and whatever it is they have in mazes, and all we saw of them for what seemed like an hour was now and then a little light from their flashlights. The sheriff decided to do some exploring on his own, and he got lost right away and was twenty minutes finding his way out, and after that he sat down and waited quietly.

When Mr. Boyd and Willie had followed one route down to its last blind alley they came back and picked up another one. They had done that three times, and they'd been gone an awfully long time on the fourth try when we heard Mr. Boyd shout. It took awhile for them to get back to us, even though they hurried and knew the way. We were all standing up waiting for them, and one look at Willie's white face was all I needed to know that they'd found the salesman's dummy, and it hadn't been a dummy.

"Is it the professor?" Grandfather asked.

Mr. Boyd nodded.

"Dead?" the sheriff asked.

Mr. Boyd nodded again.

The sheriff rubbed his hands together. "Now we can get to work," he said.

CHAPTER III

We sat around the professor's big living room, and passed the time looking up at the ceiling, some fifteen feet above us, and waiting for something to happen.

That ceiling had a history. One of Ebenezer Borg's grandsons wanted to be an artist, and Ebenezer paid the bills so the boy could go off to study in Paris and places like that. When the boy came home he naturally wanted to show his appreciation in some way, so he offered to paint one of those murals on the living room ceiling. He moved the family out of the room, and all kinds of scaffolds into it, and for weeks, according to the story, he painted away at that ceiling while not letting anyone come near the place.

When it was finished Ebenezer's wife took one look at it, and then she brought in her own painter to put about seven coats of thick paint on top of the mural.

I've heard the story from a lot of people, so it must be true, but it is also frustrating because no one seems to know what was in the painting that upset Ebenezer's wife so. Grandfather says that's a Borg family secret, and he's satisfied to leave it that way.

Professor Pesman heard the story, of course, and he liked to joke about having someone remove all the layers of paint that were put on then and afterwards, and restoring the mural. But he never did, and probably it couldn't have been done, anyway, by then, because the ceiling was full of cracks and in pretty sad shape. I liked to look at it, though, and try to imagine what that mural had been like.

Otherwise the living room was about as interesting as a cow barn with the cows out to pasture. There wasn't even a rug on the floor, just some linoleum that wasn't in much better shape than the ceiling. The few pieces of furniture looked to be something left over from Ebenezer's days, and the wall paper was so faded it was hard to figure out which were the flowers and which were the stylish ladies with umbrellas.

The professor wasn't one to surround himself with luxury, but all the other rooms in the Courthouse looked as if they could be lived in. The professor just never had any use for the living room. It would have been a fine place for dances, but no one could remember the last time anyone in the Courthouse did any dancing.

Ed Fellows paced the floor from one end of that big room to the other, grumbling that his cows had to be milked the same time every morning no matter what time he got to bed, but no one paid any attention to him. Willie sat on the floor in the corner, and cried. He didn't make any noise, but there were tears running down his face. Mr. Boyd smoked cigarette after cigarette, looking pretty mad and disgusted with the whole business. Pete Kruger sat perched on the edge of a sofa, as if he was afraid he might get dirty, and played with the white mouse. Grandfather sat on the other sofa with Nat Barlow, Grandfather whispering questions and Nat mostly shrugging his shoulders and not saying much.

Mrs. Glover moved back and forth between living room and kitchen. Her face was kind of a sickly grey, and she looked as if she might go into hysterics at any minute, but she knew a bunch of hungry men when she saw them and was holding back until she got us all fed. She brought plates of sandwiches, and coffee and cake, and then she went back for a glass of milk for me.

"Coffee stunts your growth," she said.

"I've already got my growth," I said, helping myself to a cup of coffee.

"Well, I should hope not!" she said. She poked me in the ribs, and tried to take the coffee away from me, but it isn't easy to take a hot cup of coffee away from someone who has a hold of the handle.

"Let him have the coffee," Grandfather said. "He has to stay awake to drive me home."

That started an argument about whether coffee keeps people awake, and we polished off the food and began to feel better. At least, I did.

It was nearly midnight when Sheriff Pilkins came in. He'd had flashlights scattered around in the maze, so his men could find their way to where the professor's body was, and he was all for getting his investigation finished before the professor got any colder, but his men kept getting lost in spite of his lights, and they couldn't see much anyway with only flashlights to help them, so finally he called the whole thing off until morning.

He went to the hallway, opening doors until he found a room that suited him, and then he called, "Rastin!"

Grandfather got up and nodded at me, and I followed him. The room was small, but it still had that fifteen foot ceiling, which made it look as if it were standing on end. It was so cluttered up with big heavy pieces of furniture that you couldn't move around unless you went sideways. I sat down in the corner, wondering if the sheriff would throw me out, but he didn't seem to notice me. Grandfather pounced on a rocking chair, and moved a table out of the way so he'd have plenty of space, and started rocking. It was an old wood chair without any padding, just the kind he likes.

"What are you so happy about?" the sheriff asked him.

"This chair," Grandfather said. "All the time I've known the professor,

I didn't know he had one."

The sheriff said something that sounded mostly like a snort, and found a chair for himself and got out a cigar.

"What killed him?" Grandfather asked.

"He was hit over the head," the sheriff said. "Doc says it could have been a piece of pipe. Whatever it was, the murderer took it with him."

The sheriff smoked, and Grandfather rocked.

"Got any ideas?" the sheriff asked finally.

"I've got some questions," Grandfather said.

"What are they?"

"Not what—who. Let's have Ruth Glover."

"Go get her, Johnny," the sheriff said.

Which explained why he let me stay. He figured he needed an errand boy, and I had the youngest pair of legs on the premises. I found Mrs. Glover in the kitchen, and told her the sheriff wanted to see her. She was drying a dish, and she reached out carefully to put it down and then dropped it. It bounced into the sink and broke.

"What for?" she asked.

"He'll be talking to everyone," I said. "I guess it's just a case of ladies first."

"Just a moment," she said.

She took off her apron, and then she got a compact and lipstick out of a drawer and did some quick patchwork on her face. She also gave her hair a few licks, and when she had finished she was looking maybe five minutes younger for all that, though as far as I knew she felt better, which could easily have been the important thing.

We went back to the sheriff's conference room, and he placed a chair for her and edged his way over to the far corner to concentrate on his cigar. If he had some idea about using the third degree he'd picked the wrong place for it, because the only light in the room hung ten feet above the floor and looked to be about forty watts.

Mrs. Glover sniffed the air, and made a face at the sheriff. "I don't like cigars," she said.

"I don't either," the sheriff said. "But this one was given to me, so I have to smoke it."

Grandfather cleared his throat and stepped his rocking up about one notch. "Ruth," he said, "I've known the professor since he first moved here, which is at least fifteen years longer that you've known him, and in all that time I've never once found the gate locked. Why was it locked tonight?"

"The professor wanted it locked," she said.

"Since when?"

"Since last week."

"It's been locked every night since last week?"

"Not just at night," she said. "All the time since—I think it was Wednesday."

"Do you have any idea why the professor suddenly wanted it kept locked?"

"He didn't say why. He wasn't one to explain things."

"I know," Grandfather said. "Why did you call the sheriff tonight?"

"I was scared," she said. "There've been all these robberies around, and there were lights flashing and bells ringing and people coming at us from all directions, and—"

The Sheriff snapped to attention when she mentioned the robberies. "There were only three," he said, "and they were done by some kids from Jackson, and we caught them day before yesterday."

Mrs. Glover didn't say anything.

"You didn't think to ask the professor before you called the sheriff?" Grandfather asked. "Or Boyd?"

"All I thought was that I wanted help in a hurry."

"Has the professor had any strangers visiting him in the past couple of weeks?"

"No."

"Are you sure about that?"

"No one visits in this house without my knowing about it," she said.

Grandfather turned her over to the sheriff, and he went at her with the usual stuff about whether the professor had any enemies (she supposed there were a lot of people who didn't like him, but she didn't think there were any who disliked him that much) and what was she doing between the last time anyone saw the professor alive and the time the salesman found the body (she'd been working in the kitchen, among other things, baking the chocolate cake we'd just polished off).

"All right," the sheriff said. "That'll be all," he added absently, "for now," and Mrs. Glover left the room, taking her time about it. She left the door open, and the sheriff got up and closed it.

"She doesn't look like the kind that frightens easily," the sheriff said.

"With a woman," Grandfather said, "you never know. She probably was worried about the professor suddenly wanting that gate locked."

"Who next? Nat?"

"He doesn't know anything. I've already talked with him."

"Boyd, then. Johnny—"

I brought in Mr. Boyd. He plopped into a chair, crossed his legs, and said with a grin, "I didn't do it."

The sheriff scowled. "Then you won't object to helping me find the person who did."

"Not at all. I wouldn't mind kicking his teeth in myself. He cost me a beautiful job."

"What about this business of keeping the gate locked?"

"Ask Ruth. The prof never said anything to me about it."

"Mrs. Glover looked after the house?"

"In a general way," Mr. Boyd said. "Pete is under her orders for anything she can't do herself, or doesn't want to."

"And what are your duties?"

"Very few," Mr. Boyd said. "I took notes in shorthand when the occasion required, which it rarely did. I listened sympathetically and nodded my head wisely when the prof had a theory to expound. I typed his scientific papers for him, but there weren't many of those because he never could get them published anyway. I played a bad game of cribbage on invitation, but the prof played a worse game and I sometimes had trouble to keep from beating him, so I didn't get invited often. I kept records of experiments when there were any to keep, and I gave the prof a hand when he thought he needed it." He raised his hands, palms up. "It pains me to speak of it in the past tense."

"What did you get paid for those duties?" the sheriff asked.

"A hundred and fifty a month and keep."

"Not lavish."

"I thought it was. The keep has been very good, and I didn't have any expenses. I've been here over ten years, and I have over ten thousand dollars saved."

The sheriff grunted. "One of those capitalists, eh?"

"Not on your life," Boyd said. "Just a member of the proletariat with a little money in the bank. The prof and Jerry Krohl were always needling me to get into the stock market and make a killing."

"Do you know any reason why the professor would suddenly decide to keep the gate locked?"

Mr. Boyd shook his head. "Never heard the prof mention any."

"He wasn't afraid of someone, for example?"

"I can't picture the prof being afraid of anyone."

"Any strangers called to see him lately?"

"None that I know of."

The sheriff looked around for a place to deposit his cigar butt, and couldn't find one. He held it in his hand.

"What about his mail?" Grandfather asked. "Could he have received a threatening letter?"

"I couldn't say. Pete always brought the mail to the prof. If there was anything for anyone else, the prof passed it along. Usually there wasn't."

"What were you doing between one and two o'clock today—yesterday?" the sheriff asked.

"In my room reading."

The sheriff fingered his cigar butt, and tried to think of another question. Grandfather asked, "What was the special experiment the professor was working on?"

"He didn't say."

"All right," the sheriff said. "That's all—for now."

"Can I go to bed?" Mr. Boyd wanted to know.

"Sure. But if I need you again you'll get yanked out."

"Do it gently," Mr. Boyd said. "Sometimes I'm violent when I'm woke up suddenly."

He left, closing the door, and the sheriff said, "Who's next?"

"Ed Fellows," Grandfather said. "He wants to go home."

"Let him go," the sheriff said. "He doesn't know anything you don't know, does he?"

"Why don't you ask him?" Grandfather said.

I brought Ed in, and all he knew about was the salesman being there that afternoon, and the other salesman he'd tried to get rescued that night, and he was pretty mad about the whole business. The sheriff thanked him very politely for his valuable assistance—mainly, I thought, because he was a voter and had a lot of relatives who were voters—and sent him home.

"What about Willie?" the sheriff asked. "Is there any way to get him to answer questions?"

"Johnny knows him as well as anyone does," Grandfather said. "How about it, Johnny? We know he can't talk. Can he write?"

"Never thought to try him out," I said. "Since he can' talk, I've never asked him anything that didn't have a yes or no answer."

"Supposing you find out," the sheriff said. "Wait—you'll have to be cute about this. If you were to come right out and ask him, he might be suspicious. See if you can trap him into writing something for you. Make a little detective problem out of it."

"Sure," I said. I liked Willie, but I didn't mind playing detective on him because I was pretty sure he couldn't write anyway.

I got a pencil and paper from Mrs. Glover, who was in the kitchen baking another cake—and thinking, she said, about where to get another job. Then I went to where Willie was still sitting on the floor in the corner, and trotted out the cutest trick I could think of.

"I suppose you'll be going away, now," I said to him.

He nodded. He'd stopped crying, but his big brown eyes looked plenty unhappy.

"I'd like to have your address, so I can write to you," I said.

He said, "Uh," shook his head, and gave the paper and pencil back to me.

I figured that would settle it, but then I got to wondering if he was shaking his head that he couldn't write, or that he didn't have any address.

So I asked Mrs. Glover.

"I've never seen him write anything," she said. "He does a lot of reading, or at least he spends a lot of time with books open in front of him, but I don't think he can write."

I went back and told the sheriff that the extent of Willie's literary talent remained a dark secret, and I hadn't been cute enough to penetrate it.

"Your Grandfather teaches you too many big words," he said. "What's Willie's last name?"

I didn't know, and when I made the rounds asking, neither did anyone else.

The sheriff had Pete Kruger in for questioning when I got back. Pete was sputtering around about what day something had happened.

"Mrs. Glover said you've been locking the gate since last Wednesday," the sheriff said. "Are you sure it didn't happen on Wednesday?"

"That must have been it," Pete said. "Wednesday. Because right after we got home the professor said he didn't want pests sneaking around the house to bother him, and he wanted the gate kept locked. We didn't have any lock, so I had to go back to town and buy one."

"Fine," the sheriff said. "Now tell me again just what happened in Wiston that day."

"Well, I parked on Forest Street, right across from the Paramount Theater, and the professor got out of the car and said he wouldn't be but a minute, and I told him he couldn't be more than five minutes because that was all the time there was on the meter, and just as he started to walk away someone shouted at him."

"What'd they say?" the sheriff asked.

"Just called him by name. 'Hey, Pesman.' Something like that. The professor turned, and then he opened the car door and jumped in and told me to get him out of there, so I got him out of there."

"Did you see the person who shouted at him?"

Pete shook his head.

"Do you know what the professor was going to do that would only take a minute?"

"He didn't tell me."

"After you drove away, did he ask you to drive around the block, or park somewhere else, or anything like that?"

"Nope. He told me to take him home, so I took him home. It was when we got here that he told me about the lock. And he hasn't been away from the Courthouse since then."

"You haven't told anyone else about this, have you?"

Pete looked surprised. "Nobody asked me."

"Don't, then," the sheriff said. "And yesterday afternoon you were trimming trees. We have Nat's word for that. He was with you the whole time, wasn't he?"

"Nope."

"He said he was."

"Well, I was trimming, and he was carting the branches away. Nat don't cart very fast, so he wasn't exactly with me much."

"I see," the sheriff said. "You can go to bed now, Pete. I may have some more questions for you in the morning. But wait a minute—do you know what Willie was doing yesterday afternoon?"

"Nope. I was up them trees, all the time, and Willie, he don't come outside much."

"Right," the sheriff said. "Thank you, Pete."

Pete saluted and went out, patting the mouse that was in his pocket.

The sheriff rubbed his hands—he'd gotten rid of his cigar butt while I was out detecting for him—and said, "Now we're getting somewhere."

"Where?" Grandfather asked.

"Why, we know there was some danger threatening him. We know why he started keeping the gate locked."

"Whatever it was, I'd say the professor classed it more in the category of a nuisance than a danger. He could have been mistaken, of course."

Sheriff Pilkins lit a cigarette, and meditated on this for awhile. He is not a man who is eager to turn an idea loose, once he has it cornered. He said finally, "Well, he didn't want to see this person who hailed him in town. It could be that he was afraid of him."

"Could be," Grandfather admitted. "Or if he wasn't, it could be that he should have been."

"But you don't seem to think so."

"I'm not ready to speculate on that. There are too many gaps in the facts. I've been wondering about some other things. Such as—what were these salesmen selling? The one this afternoon had a briefcase, and at least he looked legitimate, but the one tonight wasn't carrying anything."

"He could have lost his briefcase in the maze."

"I'll believe that when you find it," Grandfather said.

"What are you driving at?"

"Supposing you were a stranger in these parts, and you wanted to see the professor. But he didn't want to see you, and when you happened onto him up town he ran away. So you took a drive out to his house, and there by the road you saw some signs that said, 'Salesmen Welcome.' What would you do?"

Sheriff Pilkins straightened up with a gleam in his eyes that meant he had another idea cornered. "I'd become a salesman. So that's it. One of these salesmen was the guy that hailed the professor in town."

"Not 'was.' 'Could have been'."

"It's a good idea. Now we *are* getting somewhere."

"Where?" Grandfather asked.

The sheriff was beginning not to like that question. He said, a little bewildered and also a little irritated, "You said yourself—"

Grandfather cut him off. "Let's look at it this way. Out of the bunch you've been interviewing, who do you figure has the best alibi?"

The sheriff didn't say anything.

"Boyd was in his room reading," Grandfather said. "Ruth Glover was in the kitchen baking a cake. She had the cake to prove it, but out of all the baking I've seen done in my life, I don't recall one cake that required someone to sit and watch it while it was baking. Either Nat or Pete could have sneaked around the house and into the maze when the other wasn't looking. No one knows where Willie was. As I see it, not one of them has any alibi at all."

The sheriff still wasn't letting go of this last idea he'd cornered. "If one of those salesmen *was* the guy who hailed the professor in town—"

"You're changing the subject," Grandfather said. "All evening I've been sitting here asking myself one question. Under what circumstances would I murder a man in a maze?"

"Under what circumstances—" the sheriff worked on his cigarette until he'd raised a regular smoke screen. "All right. Under what circumstances *would* you murder a man in a maze?"

"Only when I was positive I could find my way out—fast."

That nearly produced a convulsion in the sheriff, because he had to turn loose the idea he had cornered and grab a new one, all in the same motion, and the new one seemed to be a little hard for him to hold onto. "But that means only Boyd, and Willie, and—who else? Or is there anyone else?"

"Good question," Grandfather said. "Right now I'd say it's the vital question. If you'll excuse us, I think it's time we got home. Johnny's still a growing boy, even if he doesn't think so, and he should have been in bed hours ago. Good night."

The sheriff didn't answer. I turned around to close the door after we went out, and he hadn't even moved.

CHAPTER IV

Nat Barlow decided there wasn't any point in his staying on at the Courthouse. We took him to his daughter's house in Borgville, and then we went home and found Mom waiting up for us, but that was all right, because she was worried rather than mad.

"What in the world happened?" she asked.

Grandfather was not in the mood for explanations. "I've got a feeling," he said, "that Pilkins is going to make a bad mistake."

And he went up to his room and closed the door.

This feeling of Grandfather's was not an unusual one. He had the same feeling almost every time Sheriff Pilkins had a crime to solve, and naturally he also felt that he should do everything he could to keep the sheriff from making mistakes. He'd been having these feelings for so long that I think the sheriff was uncomfortable during an investigation if Grandfather wasn't around to look over his shoulder and argue with him. Until the crime was solved there would be a kind of uneasy truce in the private war they had with each other, and then they would go at it again harder than ever, because one of them would be raving mad about the other one outsmarting him.

The sheriff enjoyed this arrangement because it got his work done, and Grandfather enjoyed it because he usually outsmarted the sheriff.

I told Mom what in the world had happened, and went to bed myself. I don't know how much sleep Grandfather got that night. He was rocking when I dozed off, and he was rocking when I woke up, around nine o'clock. His speed was only about average, which meant that he was disturbed but not frantic yet. He likes to think in his rocking chair, and you can gauge his mental state pretty accurately from how fast he rocks.

I had my breakfast, and then I went up to ask him if he'd solved the murder yet. All I got for my trouble was a dirty look, but a little later he came downstairs and asked me if I wanted to walk uptown with him.

Grandfather rarely goes over to Main Street in the morning. His habit is to get there about one o'clock on week days, and borrow the morning paper from Mr. Snubbs, who runs the Snubbs Hardware Store. He doesn't go earlier that that because he thinks it isn't right to take a man's morning paper away from him until afternoon, and though he calls it borrowing, I've never known him to return one.

Anyway, Mr. Snubbs was mighty surprised when we walked in at twenty minutes after ten. He was still reading his paper himself, but he got right up and handed it over to Grandfather.

Grandfather pushed it away. "Any strangers been around in the last couple of weeks asking questions about Charlie Pesman?" he asked.

"Not that I recall," Mr. Snubbs said.

"Last Saturday," Grandfather said, "there was a stranger in town. Good looking young fellow. He was wearing one of these fancy flowered sport shirts. Did you see him?"

Mr. Snubbs shook his head. "I heard about the professor on the radio this morning," he said. "And there's a little piece in the Detroit paper. Have you found out who did it?"

"You know Pilkins," Grandfather said.

Mr. Snubbs followed us to the door, still trying to give Grandfather his paper.

"Was it the young salesman you saw?" I asked Grandfather, when we got outside on the sidewalk.

"It was," Grandfather said, "and the fellow wasn't selling anything. He was just kind of wandering around. He came out of the Star Restaurant and walked away down Main Street, and a little later I saw him walking back on the other side of the street."

"Maybe it was his day off," I said.

"Could be. Saturday seems like a funny day for a salesman to take off, but I suppose it depends on what he was selling."

We hit every business place on Main Street, and found quite a few people who had seen this fellow, and one of the waitresses at the Star Restaurant remembered that he was real good looking, and that he'd had spaghetti and meat balls and three cups of coffee and left a very nice tip, but Grandfather didn't seem to think that this was much help. We ended up at Jake Palmer's barber shop, where Jake said that if he took the time to look at everyone walking by he'd never get any haircutting done, and Grandfather had to admit that his idea was a flop.

No one had been asking questions about the professor, and we couldn't find anyone who'd seen the young salesman do anything but eat and walk up and down Main Street.

"We'll have to go to Wiston," he said. "I'd hoped I could turn up something here, because a stranger can't do much in Borgville without a lot of people noticing. But I guess Wiston would be the logical place for anyone to make inquiries about the professor. He never came over here much."

"This afternoon?" I asked.

"I suppose," he said.

We went home for lunch, and then just as we were getting ready to leave for Wiston, Sheriff Pilkins came.

The sheriff didn't look happy. He rarely does, when he comes to our house, but this time he looked unhappier than usual. He plopped down in a chair, and said to Grandfather, "A fine help you are."

The fact that Grandfather has lost all the hair on the top of his head is somewhat compensated for by his eyebrows, which are big and bushy and very expressive. When they go up, he's puzzled about something. When they go down—look out. That time they went down.

The sheriff didn't notice, or maybe he still hasn't learned the code. "Know how many people admit to being able to find their way about in the maze?" he asked. Grandfather shook his head. "Just one, Evan Boyd, and he can't deny it because we already know that he can. Willie makes two, though he isn't able to admit it. Pete Kruger claims he'd get lost in a minute if there wasn't someone standing by, even though he has charge of keeping the hedges clipped. This hedge clipping is such a big job that Pete hires a crew of men to help him whenever it has to be done, and he says he and his men don't get lost because they clip on one side going in, and on the way out they clip on the other side and clean up as they go, and they come out all right by following the clippings. Even so, he says the professor was always around to supervise the supervising, and Boyd admits that this was true. Ruth Glover claims she's never been in the maze but once, when the professor tried an experiment with her, and she never did find her way out, so he didn't ask her again. That leaves only Nat Barlow, and everyone is certain he doesn't know the maze. He even got lost when he tried to help trim."

"What about Bill Alfred?" Grandfather asked.

The sheriff brought his thinking to a sudden stop, and stared. "Who's Bill Alford?"

"Head of the Psychology Department at Wiston College. He's been squabbling with the professor for years, but at one time they did some experiments together, and wrote about them."

The sheriff got out his notebook. "Anyone else?"

"Lyle Jones—maybe."

"Jones? The farmer Jones?"

Grandfather nodded. "He works the professor's farmland on shares."

"Don't tell me that big hick knows the maze!"

"The professor had done some experiments with him. There are people who get a kick out of that maze, you know. It's a challenge to them, and if they're exposed often enough they get addicted to it the way some people get addicted to crossword puzzles, or jigsaw puzzles, or marijuana. Temple is another one."

"I don't believe it!"

"Not the old man. His son. Junior Temple got to know the professor through his dad being the professor's attorney, and when he was younger the professor did a lot of experiments with him. Maybe he hasn't indulged since he got to be a dignified attorney himself."

"There's nothing dignified about Junior Temple, and never will be," the sheriff said. "Do you mean to tell me that these three knew the maze well enough to murder the professor in it?"

"I think Alford helped the professor design the thing. I'm not sure, though—you'll have to ask him. The others spent some time in it, but so did a lot of other people. Anyone the professor knew for five minutes got an invitation to try it out, and the professor would accommodate him as long or as frequently as his curiosity lasted. I just wanted to show you that this case isn't as simple as you thought. It's up to you to find out who knew it well enough to be able to find his way out of it."

"Thanks. There's nothing like a murder case with a million suspects."

"Not unless it's a murder case with no suspects," Grandfather said.

"Six of one and half a dozen of the other. Take those people in the Courthouse. Did you know Boyd is an ex-con with a long record? He is. Auto theft, breaking and entering, and various kinds of petty larceny. He's served seven years. He's also an alcoholic, though he does his drinking in his room at the Courthouse and no one ever sees him drunk, not even the people that live there. But all this is nothing compared with Willie's past."

He waved his hands glumly. We waited, and finally Grandfather asked, "What about Willie's past?"

"He hasn't got any. He turned up two years ago this month with a letter addressed to the professor. At least, he presented an envelope addressed to the professor, and my guess is that it was some kind of letter of introduction, or recommendation, or something. The professor hired him, but as you probably know, he only stays here summers. Shows up every year in June, and leaves in September. Boyd thinks he doesn't like cold weather and goes south for the winter. Where he goes, or where he comes from—or where he originally came from—nobody knows."

"Who inherits the professor's money?" Grandfather asked.

"Everybody," the sheriff said. "And nobody. All employees working for him at the time of his death get this month's pay, and an additional month's severance pay, plus a thousand dollars."

"Even Nat?"

"Nat Barlow was an employee at the time of his death, so of course he gets what the others get. Fifty thousand dollars goes to the professor's stepdaughter. I'd forgotten that he'd ever married."

Grandfather's eyebrows did acrobatics. "It was—let's see, about 1951 or 1952. His housekeeper was a young woman who'd lost her husband in the war. I think it was mainly on account of her daughter that the professor married her. The daughter was a cute kid—oh, maybe eight or nine—and the professor loved children. The marriage only lasted a few months, and then the woman left, taking the kid with her of course, and got a divorce. I never heard the professor mention her again, but he talked about the kid once in a while."

"The professor paid a cash settlement in lieu of alimony, and no one knows where they went or where they might be now. Temple is grumbling about having to find the girl. Well—the stepdaughter gets fifty thousand. The residue, which Temple thinks will amount to about four hundred thousand, goes to a professor at Landsdorf College, down in Ohio or to his children if he's not living. Because, Pesman says in his will, he had faith—whatever that means."

"Professor of what?"

"Professor—oh, you mean the guy that gets the loot. No one knows."

"What's his name?"

"Andrew Vaughan."

"What about the salesman?"

"There's no trace of either of them. I haven't even been able to find out for sure what kind of cars they were driving—and at least half a dozen of you dunces stood around one of the cars for an hour yesterday afternoon."

Grandfather's eyebrows dipped again. "May I point out that one of those dunces was your own deputy? Your department is performing with its usual efficiency."

That the sheriff didn't explode was a good indication of how low he was feeling. "I figure the second salesman is out of it," he said. "If he'd murdered the professor, he certainly wouldn't have been idiot enough to come back later and get lost in the maze. The first one, the young fellow who said he found a body, is the one I'd like to talk with. Have you any idea what the odds are against anyone finding the professor by accident in that maze?"

Grandfather shook his head.

"I guess about a thousand to one."

"He wasn't exactly acting suspicious," Grandfather said. "He reported finding the body to the first officer he saw, and he only went back into the maze after we convinced him that it wasn't a body."

"Boyd says a stranger wouldn't be able to find his way that far into the maze in the first place, and wouldn't be able to find his way out in the second place, and then there are those thousand-to-one odds. I don't suppose you'd want to guess about who did it."

"I don't suppose I would."

"If you think of anything else, give me a call."

"Likewise," Grandfather said.

The sheriff's face reddened, but he managed to leave without slamming the screen door.

"Wiston?" I said to Grandfather.

"Wiston," Grandfather said.

Wiston is a bit larger than Borgville. To be exact about it, it is 24,417 people larger, or it was when they took the 1960 census, when Wiston was counted at 25,228 and Borgville at 811. The Wiston paper likes to call the place a metropolis, but most of the Borgville people have other names for it, of which *den of iniquity* is one of the milder ones. I wouldn't want to leave the impression that Wiston is a bad town, but only that we in Borgville feel that there's room for improvement.

I parked across from the Paramount Theater, where Pete Kruger said he parked the professor's car that day, and Grandfather and I did a quick survey of the business places. We turned up a very curious fact.

The professor rarely went to Borgville, but everyone there knew him and knew all about him. He often went to Wiston, and we only found three people there who recognized his name, and that was because they'd heard about the murder. In justice to the people of Wiston, I must point out that this was before the evening paper came out. If the people had had a chance to read about the murder in the paper, we might have had five or six who'd heard of the professor.

"There should be a law," Grandfather said, "against towns having more than a thousand people. A town of a thousand is big enough to serve any rational need."

I told him that people were probably more interested in needs that weren't rational, and he said something like that had occurred to him, too.

We walked over to the Temple & Temple law offices, and Grandfather, who knew Norman Temple, Senior, from way back, didn't have any trouble getting an interview. The two Temples, Old Man and Junior, had their desks back-to-back in a big room, and as we went in they did a synchronized swivel in their chairs to face us. Junior was only a couple of years out of law school. He was short and skinny and he looked like a bright high school kid who'd never make the football team. He wore thick glasses with black frames and a bow tie that kept getting a roller coaster ride over his Adam's apple. Those that knew him said he was plenty smart, and would make a good lawyer if he ever got over being scared of people.

His father had never been scared of anyone. He was built like a lumber jack, and when he got going in a court room, he reminded people of Daniel Webster, though as far as I know none of them really knew what Daniel Webster looked like. Old Man Temple was proud of his son, but I think a little disgusted with him, too, because when he introduced him he would always say, "He looks like his mother," which wasn't necessary.

It was Professor Pesman who said that it was good psychology for Old Man Temple to have a big room for his office, because any client would be afraid to be in a small room with him.

Junior got up to get chairs for us, but Grandfather waved him back to his seat. "Just one thing," he said. "All the time I knew the professor it never occurred to me to ask, but now I'm curious. Where did he get his money?"

The two Temples looked at each other, holding what seemed to be a long-distance legal conference. "It's no special secret that I know of," Old Man Temple said. "He inherited it. From an uncle, I believe."

"I figured it was something like that," Grandfather said. "When he came here he was right away the wealthiest man in Borg County, and he didn't get that way teaching. At least, all the teachers I know say he didn't. Thanks."

We went back to my jalopy. "Home?" I asked.

"I suppose so," Grandfather said. But he changed his mind before I got the motor started, and told me to stop at the Courthouse. I resigned myself to a late supper, and we drove off.

Externally the Courthouse hasn't changed much since Ebenezer Borg's time. It's a big, well-built brick building with a little dome on the top, and it's in better condition than some buildings I know that are a hundred years younger. Professor Pesman spent a lot of money getting it into first class shape. He even had the bricks sand-blasted, or some such thing, to make them look—well, almost new.

There were five cars in the Courthouse drive when we got there— Professor Pesman's, which I suppose was now the property of Andrew Vaughan, or would be when the law got around to letting him have it, two patrol cars from the Sheriff's Department, a State Police car, and one that I didn't recognize. Mrs. Glover waved us on into the dining room, and there at the dining room table Mr. Boyd was talking with a man I'd never seen before.

He introduced us. "Jerry Krohl," he said. "Bill Rastin and his grandson, Johnny."

I knew right away that Jerry Krohl was some kind of salesman, from the glad way he bounced up and shook hands with us. Then I remembered that he was the professor's broker. He was tall, and maybe a little on the plump side, though it didn't show much because of his height. His clothes looked like something out of the window of one of those fancy men's stores, and even his bow tie looked good. It wasn't like Junior Temple's—it *fit*.

"Jerry has a problem," Mr. Boyd said.

"That so?" Grandfather said.

Mr. Boyd nodded. He presented quite a contrast to Mr. Krohl, because he had on his old robe again, though this time he had pants on under it. He still wore his contented look, too, and if he had any problems of his own they didn't show. "Tell Mr. Rastin about it, Jerry," he said. "Maybe he can help you."

"It isn't exactly my problem," Krohl said, "but it worries me. The professor was doing some speculating, and he picked a lemon. That is, it was a smart speculation up to last week, and he had a nice profit—a darned nice profit—in the stock, but he wouldn't sell. Then it started down. He lost all his profit, and more, and he still wouldn't sell. Said he'd never sold a stock at a loss yet, but then, he never speculated before either. Up to this year he never bought anything but blue chips. Day before yesterday this stock dropped four points, and I came out yesterday to see if I could talk him into selling. I couldn't. It held steady yesterday, but today it's down two, and I'm afraid the bottom will drop right out of it."

"It's no concern of mine," Mr. Boyd said, "even if it goes down to zero. And there's not much chance of getting the prof to sell now. Wherever he is, he's not worried about money."

"*Someone* should be worried about it," Krohl said. "Someone is losing money every time this stock takes another dip, and there isn't any sense in it."

"It'd probably be up to the executor of his estate," Grandfather said.

"I know. Do you know who it is?"

Grandfather shook his head. "I just talked to Norm Temple, but I didn't think to ask him."

"If that's all that's bothering you," Mr. Boyd said, "I can help you out. It's Junior Temple."

Krohl stared at him. "Nonsense!"

"That's what Pilkins said."

"Norm's health hasn't been good," Grandfather said. "I heard he was turning a lot of his work over to Junior. And the professor always liked Junior, on account of Junior being interested in the maze. So I suppose it's possible."

"If I have to get permission from Junior Temple to sell this stock, I might as well forget it," Krohl said.

"I don't know whether the executor has the authority to sell a stock or not," Grandfather said. "You'll have to ask him."

"Oh, he has the authority, all right," Krohl said. "But Junior Temple would never use it. It would take him six months just to make up his mind to say no, and by that time—"

"By that time maybe the heir will have taken over, and you can deal with him," Mr. Boyd said. "Try talking with Old Man Temple first. If you can convince him you won't have to worry about Junior."

"I suppose that's the answer," Krohl said. "I'll try, anyway. Nice to meet you, Mr. Rastin. If you're ever interested in investments, give me a call."

Grandfather promised to do just that, and Krohl went out, pausing in the kitchen to maybe toss an investment or two at Mrs. Glover.

"What's the sheriff up to?" Grandfather asked Boyd.

"Steve Carling thinks he's found something important. Sergeant Reichel is here, and he's not so sure. The sheriff is trying to make up his mind."

"Where are they?"

"Out in the maze. But they aren't encouraging kibitzers."

"Come on, Johnny," Grandfather said.

The sheriff had probably gotten tired of having to ask Mr. Boyd or Willie to rescue his deputies, and he had a white tape laid down in the maze. All we had to do was follow it, but even with a tape to follow I felt uneasy going through the maze. The paths were maybe six, seven feet wide, but there was that hedge towering over you on either side, and if you got lost you were really lost and the professor's special gimmick—which was the woven wire fence inside the hedges—wasn't calculated to reassure you any. The professor wasn't having any of his experiments ruined by one of his specimens sneaking through a thin spot in the hedge. You rarely saw the fence, but if there was a place where there wasn't one I hadn't found it any of the times the professor had me running in the maze.

The paths were graveled, and though the gravel was packed down it still made some noise when you walked on it, if you weren't careful. The sheriff heard us long before we got to him, and he roared, "Who the devil is that?"

Grandfather marched straight ahead without answering, and we rounded a corner and found the sheriff with two of his deputies and Sergeant Reichel, of the State Police.

The sheriff wasn't pleased to see us. "What do you want now?" he said.

Grandfather shook hands with Sergeant Reichel, and passed the time of day with him for a couple of minutes while the sheriff glared and the deputies shifted their feet and looked embarrassed.

Steve Carling came trotting up. He said, "There isn't anything—oh."

"It's just Borgville's super snooper," the sheriff said.

Grandfather went on talking with Sergeant Reichel.

"I didn't find anything," Steve Carling said.

"I didn't think you would," the sheriff said.

"He usually doesn't," Grandfather said.

The sheriff's face underwent some interesting changes. He reared back, and thundered, "Now look here—"

"I suppose you've solved the crime," Grandfather said.

"As a matter of fact," the sheriff said, "I have."

Grandfather blinked, and turned to sergeant Reichel. "It's possible," the sergeant said. "I don't think it's likely, but it's possible."

"Who did it?" Grandfather asked.

"Nobody."

"Nobody? You call that a solution?"

"Come here."

We followed the sheriff around a turn, to a place where most of the path was taped off. The sheriff tiptoed around it. "This is where the body was," he said. He took another turn, and stopped at the end of a hedge where a small square was taped off. "Look," he said.

It was one of the few places in the maze where you could see the fence. The hedge stopped a foot or so before the end of the row, and the fence, and the end fence post, stuck out beyond it. The sheriff squatted down and pointed to the fence post. "Look."

We looked. For a moment I thought the post was rusted, but then I saw that something was smeared on it.

"Blood," the sheriff said. "And there's blood on the path. We've also found a few blood spots between here and where the body was found."

"Are you trying to say this post is the pipe the professor was hit with?" Grandfather asked.

"Not 'was hit with.' Hit. This is the pipe he hit."

Grandfather scratched his head, and looked around at Sergeant Reichel. The Sergeant shrugged his shoulders.

"It would take quite a blow to do to a head what the professor had done to his," the sergeant said. "I'd want the opinion of a good pathologist. Doc Phillips is no good on a problem like this."

"What does the Doc say?" Grandfather asked.

"We haven't been able to get a hold of him."

"Are you sure that stuff is blood?"

"We're having it tested."

"I didn't see the professor's head," Grandfather said. "But my opinion would be that a man would have to be traveling pretty fast if a collision with that post was to give him more than a headache. And the professor never moved fast. He wasn't built to move fast."

"I didn't say he collided with it," the sheriff said. "Obviously he wouldn't have struck his head there if he collided with it. He fell, and hit it as he was falling. There's a lot of blood on the ground here."

Grandfather bent over and squinted at the post again.

"Well, what do you think?" the sheriff asked.

"As a fairy story it isn't bad," Grandfather said. "But it's not the sort of thing that gets a man reelected for sheriff."

"Now see here!"

"No point in arguing about it," Sergeant Reichel said. "We'll see what Doc says, and we'll see how the stuff tests, and then—then we'll see. It doesn't sound very plausible to me, but the professor was an old man, and I suppose it could have happened that way."

"He was a hard-headed old man," Grandfather said. "He'd have had to be running, and pitch right into the post, and I don't think that's possible. If he hit it at all he hit it rounding this corner, and even if he was running, which is something I've never known the professor to do, he'd have slowed down for the corner. What do you figure made him fall?"

"I don't know," the sheriff said. "He was an old man, you know."

"He was more than twenty years younger than I am. Maybe he tripped over one of those big lumps of gravel."

He kicked the gravel, and turned and marched away. I followed him, and we found our way out of the maze, following the tape, and circled the house to get back to my jalopy.

"Pilkins is an idiot," Grandfather said.

"Sure," I said. "The professor would have had to be doing the Twist to fall and hit that post."

"Also, if the professor's head was mashed as badly as they say it was, he didn't get up and walk a dozen feet."

"He did if his head was made of rubber," I said. "And it must be."

"Why do you say that?"

"When it hits something, it bounces."

"What are you talking about?"

"Didn't you notice where the blood was? Almost in the center of the path. I was wondering while we were there how a man could fall and hit that post, and then do all his bleeding so far away."

"Johnny," Grandfather said, "any time you want to run for sheriff, you've got my vote."

CHAPTER V

The next day, Thursday, Grandfather suddenly remembered that he had unfinished business at his house in Wiston. We went over there early and spent the entire morning cleaning up, and then Grandfather decided that the house needed painting inside and out, not to mention some plastering here and there, and he had to arrange for some estimates, and with one thing and another it was the middle of the afternoon before we were able to start back to Borgville.

We detoured around to the County Building, just to see if, as Grandfather put it, Sheriff Pilkins had shaken any of the cobwebs out of his brains. The sheriff wasn't in. The young deputy who was in charge had overheard some to the things Sheriff Pilkins has said about Grandfather in his less restrained moments, and he had the idea that both Grandfather and I were undesirable characters.

So we drove out to the Courthouse, and there we walked in on a conference between Mr. Boyd and Mrs. Glover. They were trying to decide if they should stay on there any longer, and if so, how much longer. Willie was present, but only in a listening capacity, of course.

"That's something you should take up with the executor," Grandfather said.

"I did," Mr. Boyd said disgustedly. "I asked Junior point blank: 'Do you want the four of us out of here, or should we stay on for awhile?' We're to be paid our regular salaries through June, and I figured this put us at his disposal at least to the end of the month. He thought about it for awhile, and then he gave out with some wherefores and whereas-on-the-other-hands, and when he got through talking I didn't know whether we were to stay here until next year, or we should move out yesterday. I hope I never have to ask another question of a lawyer."

"Not all lawyers are like that," Grandfather said. "Junior is something special. He's the bookish type. He should be with one of those big law firms where they have one man to do all the studying for the others. He'd be a whiz at that. But his dad's intent on him being his father's son, and he'll make a practicing attorney out of him or ruin the boy in the process. It's kind of a shame."

"It's sure a hardship on the people who have to do business with him," Mr. Boyd said.

"What's the news from Pilkins?"

"Oh, he's walking on clouds. He found some blood on a fence post, and the test proves it was the prof's blood, and the sheriff figures the prof fell and busted his head, and he can forget about finding a murder and get back to his pinochle game."

"What do you think?" Grandfather asked.

"Well, I went out and had a look at the post. Naturally I hope the sheriff's right, but considering the layout there I don't see how anyone but a snake could have hit it head-on. Whatever the prof ran into got him right smack on top of his head, you know."

"I didn't know," Grandfather said. "But I doubted that he could have killed himself by hitting any part of his head on that post."

Mrs. Glover took a notion to feed us, then, and we settled for one piece of pie and a glass of milk apiece, and then we excused ourselves and left them to go on with their conference. From what Mr. Boyd had said about the sheriff I expected Grandfather to be at least mad enough to slam the car door, but he didn't. He didn't even say anything until we were almost to Borgville, and then he started to talk about the professor.

"Charlie Pesman wasn't a very likable person," he said. "In a lot of ways he was like a spoiled kid with an expensive toy. That's what his maze was, actually—a darned expensive toy and he was likely to have a grudge against anyone who wouldn't play with it his way. He liked to be called 'professor' but I don't believe he ever was one. That's the top of the ladder for college teachers, and even if he did teach psychology at the college I doubt that he made it very far up the ladder. He had amazing intelligence, but he never used his brains for anything but thinking up new games to play."

"I thought he was a crackpot," I said.

"Lots of geniuses are crackpots," Grandfather said. "The professor had some wonderful ideas. Trouble was, he never kept after one of them long enough to accomplish anything. He was a genius who couldn't concentrate. It's just as if this Vincy fellow that painted 'The Last Supper' had spend his life working on ten thousand different pictures, and never finished a one. No matter how good a painter he was, no one ever would have heard of him. If the professor could have concentrated, he could have done one or two or three worthwhile things, and he'd have been considered a great man."

"With all that money, he didn't have to concentrate," I said.

"Maybe that was the trouble," Grandfather said. "Maybe the money spoiled him. There was something childish about the way he played with that big toy of his, and kept whole filing cabinets full of silly records about how long it took this person and that rat to find the way out of his maze.

I think there was a mean streak in him, too. He liked to scare people, and embarrass them, and from some of the things he did to his animals—and people—I used to wonder if maybe he wouldn't have been right at home in one of those medieval torture chambers. Still, for all his meanness I don't think he was as mean as the man that murdered him. I don't aim to let the murderer get away with it."

By that time we'd pulled up in front of our house. Grandfather got out, and closed the door of my jalopy very carefully. "Besides," he said, "he was a friend of mine."

A little later the painting estimates started to come in from Wiston and in no time at all Grandfather was in a rage. He practically ruptured the telephone talking to one of the contractors. "I just wanted the house painted!" he roared. "For that money I could tear it down and put up a new one."

When he got the fourth estimate, which was the highest one, he walked over to talk to Bob Meyers. Borgville doesn't have any painters, but there are a couple of men who'll work at it part-time, if they're asked politely enough, and Bob was one of them. Grandfather worked out a deal with him to arrange to take his vacation starting the end of the week, and paint the house, and Grandfather seemed more cheerful when he came back. His cheerfulness didn't last long, though. Right after supper Sheriff Pilkins came, and when Grandfather saw him drive up he told me to tell the sheriff he wasn't available, and he went upstairs to his room.

I told the sheriff, and the sheriff sat down in the living room, and crossed his legs, and perched his hat on one knee. "What does he want me to do?" he asked. "Apologize?"

"I'll ask him," I said.

I went upstairs and told Grandfather that the sheriff wanted to apologize. Grandfather said he'd believe it when he heard it, but he did come down after making the sheriff wait for awhile. Grandfather likes to keep Sheriff Pilkins waiting. He says it teaches the sheriff self control.

"Well, you were right," the sheriff said.

"Then the professor didn't run into the fence post."

The sheriff shook his head. "Reichel brought in a couple of doctors, including one from the University of Michigan. They found some little pieces of rust in the wound, so the professor was hit with a rusty pipe. The fence post isn't rusty. They also found some bruises and other things, and they say the professor was hit on the head by a powerful blow, and he fell face down onto the gravel. They also say he was killed instantly, and they think it happened right there by that post. Then the person who did it smeared blood on the post, somehow, and moved the body around the next corner. None of which makes any sense to me."

"It probably made sense to the murderer," Grandfather said.

"Now I'm right back where I started. Who did it?"

"If I were you," Grandfather said, "I'd stop worrying about that for awhile and ask myself why."

"I'm willing," the sheriff said. "Why?"

"Take Evan Boyd. Any reason for him to kill his boss?"

Sheriff Pilkins shook his head. "He gets a thousand, of course, but I don't think he knew that. At least, all of them claim they didn't know about it. All except Willie, of course—it's hard to say what he knows. Temple feels certain that the professor never told anyone what was in his will. The only thing Boyd would have thought he was accomplishing was to do himself out of a job, and he liked his job. He says he liked it, anyway."

"Mrs. Glover?"

"Same reasoning. She's been there a long time—since not long after the professor's wife left him. She liked her job, too."

"Willie?"

"There I couldn't say," the sheriff said. "As far as I can find out, the professor got along real well with him. Favored him over the others in some ways. On the other hand, Willie may not have thought much of his job, since he only worked here three month out of the year. I just don't know."

"Pete Kruger?"

"Same situation as Boyd and Mrs. Glover, except for one thing. The professor and Pete did have a spat last week. Pete left a cage open and a white rat got out. So the professor banished Pete from the laboratory and brought in Nat Barlow to look after the animals. Pete was upset about it, but everyone thought it was a temporary arrangement, kind of a punishment for Pete. The professor thought punishment was good psychology."

"Was Pete upset to do murder?"

"Pete wasn't much of a thinker, but even he would see that he'd lose his animals permanently if the professor died."

"Nat Barlow?"

"I wouldn't even consider him," he sheriff said.

"That takes care of them individually. How about collectively?"

"You'll have to explain that."

"Here we have a household with five men and one woman. Scratch out Nat and Pete. Scratch out Willie, too. That leaves the professor, and Boyd, and Ruth Glover. A lot of people have thought for a long time that Ruth was more than a housekeeper in the house, but there's been some difference of opinion as to whether she was being more than a housekeeper to the professor or to Boyd. I wouldn't want to express an opinion one way or the other, but I've seen worse messes develop out of less."

"I'll look into it," the sheriff said. "Boyd could have been interested in eliminating the professor for various reasons. Is that what you mean?"

Grandfather nodded. "Now—what about the outsiders?"

"Well, there were those two salesmen."

"It's a little hard to fit motives onto people when you don't know who they are," Grandfather said. "What about the others? Junior Temple, for example."

"All he gets out of it is the job of executor, and somehow I can't see him swinging a piece of rusty pipe. He'd have polished it up first."

"His father?"

"You might reason that he wanted his son to get some executor experience, but I hate to think what the County Attorney would say if I offered him that for evidence."

"Has the law firm been handling any business transactions for the professor?"

"I can find out," the sheriff said, scribbling in his notebook. "But you know yourself that Norm Temple would rather be caught dead than doing something dishonest, and Junior wouldn't have the nerve."

"That's as good a motive for murder as you'll ever find," Grandfather said.

"What's that?"

"Norm would rather be caught dead than doing something dishonest. Suppose the professor caught him?"

The sheriff muttered something under his breath, and underlined what he'd written.

"Jerry Krohl?" Grandfather said.

"He's just lost his best client. Also, he's never been in the maze. The professor even tried to bribe him with a stock order, once, and he wouldn't take it."

"What was the chance of his making free with the professor's brokerage account?"

"He doesn't handle any money," the sheriff said. "He's just a salesman taking orders. The accounts are kept at the Detroit office. Strobel, Ross, Beal and Larkins. It's a big firm, and anyone making free with its accounts would have to fool a battery of IBM machines and a regiment of auditors."

"Have you been buying stocks?" Grandfather asked.

"Once in a while."

Grandfather made a face. "Lyle Jones?"

"There's about a hundred and twenty-five acres left of the old Borg farm. Jones's dad farmed that on shares for the professor, from the time the professor bought the Borg place, and Jones took over when his dad retired. They have eighty acres of their own, of course. Father and son, they've been working for the professor for better than twenty-five years without a whisper of any trouble, which is a pretty good record."

"It's a remarkable record," Grandfather said, "especially considering that the professor was a party to it. Bill Alford?"

"When the professor first came here, they used to get together and talk psychology. They tell me Alford is a good teacher and has a good reputation. He's well-liked around Wiston College. It didn't take him long to decide that Pesman was a nut, and they haven't seen much of each other for years. Also, he has an iron-clad alibi."

"At least once a year," Grandfather said, "Alfred would bring a bunch of students over and turn them loose in the maze. He thought it was good for them to get acquainted with the rat's point of view. Naturally the professor liked that."

"Naturally. It was a good day whenever he got anyone into that maze. Did I tell you he was always after me to give it a try?"

"Me, too," Grandfather said. "Every time I went to see him. Who else is there?"

"Only the two that really matter. The stepdaughter and this Professor Andrew Vaughan."

"Has Norm gotten in touch with Vaughan?"

"He wrote him yesterday morning, as soon as he heard. Asked him to telephone. He hasn't yet, but then—he probably hasn't gotten the letter yet."

"That's the way Norm does things," Grandfather said. "He writes a letter, which only costs a nickel, so the other fellow will have to pay for the telephone call."

"The letter won't even cost him a nickel," the sheriff said. "He'll charge it to the estate. He could charge a phone call to the estate, too. Either way, Vaughan pays."

"True," Grandfather said. "But where money is concerned, Norm Temple doesn't reason things out. He just acts naturally. Where were we? Vaughan and the stepdaughter. Has Norm located the stepdaughter?"

"He doesn't even know where to start."

"Just give it to the papers that there's fifty thousand dollars here waiting for her. She'll turn up."

"It's an idea. But I can't see that the 'why' gets us any further than the 'who.' As far as we know, the people with the best motives weren't even in this state at the time of the murder. The people with the best opportunity haven't any motives at all, unless we count this love triangle thing, and I suppose I'd better count it. There isn't much else, unless one of the professor's silly psychological tricks has made someone mad at him, and that lets in half of Borg County."

"It seems to me that you have a lot of facts worth thinking about,"

Grandfather said.

"Then I guess I'd better go home and think," the sheriff said. And he did. At least he went home.

Grandfather went back up to his rocking chair, to do some thinking of his own, but when I looked in on him later he wasn't working very hard at it.

"Did you hear anyone say exactly how old this stepdaughter is now?" he asked.

"Not that I remember," I said.

"I figure she's somewhere between eighteen and twenty-two," Grandfather said.

"I guess that makes her old enough to murder a man," I said. "Is that what you wanted to know?"

"Not exactly," Grandfather said. "If there's been a young woman hanging around the Courthouse no one noticed her. I was wondering if she could have a husband involved in this. One of those salesmen, maybe, since they're the only strangers in on it so far. Which one do you think it is?"

"For her sake, I hope it's the youngest one," I said. "Are you going to tell the sheriff?"

"It's the kind of wild hunch that would appeal to him," Grandfather said. "But maybe we should let him get a little work done before we send him off on another tangent. There's one thing more. This second salesman—the one that was lost in the maze at night. Would you say he maybe looked a little like a college professor?"

"I suppose maybe he did," I said.

"I thought he had that kind of dusty, dried-up look, like some of those professors at Wiston College that get turned out at night when the library closes. Well, it seemed to me that this salesman looked like a college professor, and then I find that the principal heir is a college professor. What do you think of that?"

"Wow!" I said. "Sheriff Pilkins—"

Grandfather grinned, and stepped up his rocking a little. "The implications would drive Pilkins nuts," he said. "Two strangers in the case and one of them turning out to be the husband of the stepdaughter, and the other one the other heir in person. Pilkins would lock both of them up, and swallow the key. I'm almost tempted to suggest it, just to watch the expression on his face."

"Then you don't think it's possible?" I asked.

"Johnny, anything is possible. I was just sitting here cogitating on the amount of progress that's been made so far. Except for proving that the professor didn't run into a post, which I didn't believe for a moment, I can't see that there's been any. No wonder Pilkins is ready to grasp at straws—or fence posts. I've been thinking that if Norm Temple doesn't hear from this man Vaughan pretty soon, someone ought to go down to Ohio and see what sort of person this principal heir is, and I just might do it myself. And if I was to call on him and find out he *was* the salesman—well, it's rare moments like those that make life worth living."

CHAPTER VI

The next morning at the breakfast table I asked Grandfather when we were going to Ohio.

"Know anyone in these parts that's been to Landsdorf College?" Grandfather asked.

I didn't.

"If we could find someone, maybe he'd have one of those yearbooks. It might have a picture of Professor Vaughan."

"On the other hand," I said, "maybe he wouldn't, and if he did it might not."

"You're just angling for an excuse to drive a hundred miles."

"It's only ninety," I said. "I looked it up last night."

"That's eighty-nine miles too far to drive out of curiosity," Grandfather said. "Temple should be hearing from Vaughan practically any minute."

But he didn't. Sheriff Pilkins didn't accomplish anything that day, either—at least, he didn't accomplish anything that he wanted to brag about, or he would have been by to see Grandfather. Things around our house were quiet to the point of being dull, and the next day, Saturday, was no improvement. Grandfather slipped back into his usual routine. He went over to Main Street after lunch, and borrowed Mr. Snubbs' morning paper, and read it sitting on the bench in front of Jake Palmer's barber shop. Nat Barlow, being fresh out of gainful employment, sat on the bench beside him and watched the cars go by, and when some men congregated there to talk about Professor Pesman's murder Grandfather listened and didn't say anything.

Saturday evening Grandfather telephoned Norman Temple and the lawyer told him that there hadn't been any reply to his letter. They had a long talk about this, Grandfather insisting that he had nothing against the U.S. mails, and that all things considered a postage stamp could easily be as much of a bargain as one could find anywhere, but in an emergency people had been known to use the telephone with good results. Mr. Temple wasn't easy to convince, but Grandfather managed it, and he said, "Let me know how you make out. I'll be waiting."

We waited, and a little later Mr. Temple called back. He had placed a person-to-person call to Andrew C. Vaughan in Windalia, Ohio, which was where Landsdorf College was, and the operator there had told him that no Andrew C. Vaughan was listed. From this the lawyer concluded that Mr. Vaughan had moved away from Windalia, and that the letter that had already been mailed would either be forwarded to him or returned to the sender. If the latter, all concerned could take council when the letter came back, and decide what to do next.

"Maybe he doesn't use his initial," Grandfather said.

Temple thought of that. There wasn't any kind of Andrew Vaughan listed in Windalia.

"I suppose it is remotely possible that he's there, but doesn't have a telephone," Grandfather said.

Mr. Temple said triumphantly that this was why he wrote a letter in the first place. Grandfather snorted and hung up.

"If he'd started earlier, he could have tried to get him at the college," Grandfather said. "But now nothing can be done about that until Monday morning, and if we wait that long—will that jalopy of yours get us as far as Windalia, Ohio?"

"It sure will," I said.

"And back?"

"If it'll get us there, it'll get us back."

Grandfather didn't seem to share my confidence, but after he'd meditated for a time he announced that we would leave for Windalia, Ohio the following afternoon, and if all went well—meaning, if my jalopy didn't fall apart—we'd return on Monday.

I said fine, and hurried over to the Borgville Service Station to buy three gallons of motor oil to take along. My jalopy is a nice car, and it runs fine, but it has one or two expensive habits that I haven't been able to break it of.

We started out right after Sunday dinner. It was another hot day, and of course Grandfather insisted on riding with all the windows up, so it was a good thing that I had to stop every now and then to add oil, because it gave me a chance to get the car cooled out. I took my time driving—Grandfather likes to have a good look at the country when he goes to a place he's never been before—and it was nearly five o'clock when we reached Windalia.

We stopped at a little restaurant just inside the city limits, and Grandfather marched right over to the telephone booth to look at the phone book. There, in the usual block letters, he found the name Andrew C. Vaughan, with a street address and a telephone number.

Grandfather did not know quite what to make of this. "If it'd been Pilkins," he said, "I'd say he probably got confused and called some town in Alaska by mistake. But Norm Temple is no dunce. The operator must have made a mistake."

He called the number, and got no answer. We had a light supper, on

Grandfather's favorite menu of hamburgers and chili, and then he tried again with the same result.

A couple of blocks up the street we found ourselves a motel, and after we'd checked in and I'd given my jalopy another swallow of oil, we went out to have a look at Windalia, Ohio.

It reminded me a lot of Wiston, Michigan. It was a college town that had grown up, so that part of the town was sleepy-looking streets with big elm trees and old houses plastered with fancy ornaments, and part of it was modern, with a few factories, and whole neighborhoods of new houses that looked to have hatched out only yesterday and with no trees at all. Landsdorf College was a little like Wiston College, though it didn't seem quite as large. It had some old buildings that could have been dedicated by President Millard Fillmore, and some new buildings that looked as if they might head for outer space before anyone got around to dedicating them, and quite a few of the in-between kinds. There didn't seem to be many students around, and it was just at that moment that Grandfather had a horrible thought.

"Johnny!" he said. "It's summer!"

I know Grandfather well enough to know that he would not make a remark like this in the middle of June in the hope of starting an argument. Even so, it seemed like a funny thing to say. "I guess so," I said, "and just think—only yesterday it was spring."

"School is out," Grandfather said. "College is out, too, for most students, and this professor is probably gone for the summer."

"Not necessarily," I said. "Some professors teach in the summer. Maybe he's only gone for the weekend."

"I knew from the start that this trip would be a waste of time and money," Grandfather said. "But you nagged me into it."

I don't remember just when I learned never to argue with Grandfather. I guess I sort of grew up knowing that of all the ways anyone can think of to waste time that is the one way that will waste the most of it. I asked him if he wanted to start home right away, and he said as long as we were there we might as well see what we could find out, so we went back to our hotel. He telephoned three more times during the evening, and by the time he went to bed he was so mad he wasn't speaking to me.

First thing in the morning he telephoned again. Still no answer, so we went over to Landsdorf College to see if anyone there knew anything about Professor Andrew C. Vaughan.

At the information desk in the Administration Building there was a real young girl who looked too fresh to even be a freshman. Grandfather asked her about Andrew Vaughan, and she checked over a list of teachers, smiled sweetly, and said there wasn't one by that name.

"Maybe he's retired," Grandfather said. "Do you have a list of retired teachers?"

She didn't

"I know he used to teach here," Grandfather said, "and he's still listed in the telephone directory. How would I go about finding out something about him?"

The girl wasn't equipped to handle questions like that, so she passed it—and us—along to a higher administrative level. We were escorted into an office, and there was a little old lady who hadn't even been a graduate student since the first World War. Unfortunately she hadn't been on the job any longer than the girl in the lobby. She checked a list of names and looked through a college directory, and finally told Grandfather that Andrew Vaughan wasn't teaching at the summer session and hadn't taught there the previous year.

"Try five years ago," Grandfather suggested.

That worked. Andrew C. Vaughan had been a professor of English, and what's more, chairman of the English Department.

Grandfather looked at me and scratched his head. "I can't see that it helps us much," he said. "It's not much more than we already knew."

At that moment we were rescued by a kindly-looking old gentleman who turned out to be the President of Landsdorf College, though he didn't stand on any formality because he was wearing a short-sleeved shirt without a necktie. The fact that it was another hot day and there wasn't a whiff of air conditioning in that building could have had something to do with it.

"Andy Vaughan?" he said. "Andy retired a year ago. And," he added, just as Grandfather's face brightened with the thought that he was at last getting somewhere, "he died last April. The twelfth, I think it was. He was a splendid gentleman, and we all miss him."

He scooted off to do whatever it is that a college president does, and left Grandfather in too much of a daze to even thank the lady who'd tried to help us. I thanked her for him, and gently led Grandfather outside.

We got in the jalopy, and I automatically started to roll the windows up, thinking that we could, by hurrying, get to Borgville in time for a late lunch.

"Why wasn't Temple's letter returned to him?" Grandfather asked.

"We could go over to the post office and ask," I said. "They probably haven't gotten around to it yet."

"Why is his name in the phone book?" Grandfather asked.

"That's easy," I said. "He just died a couple of months ago, and there hasn't been a new phone book since then."

"Why," Grandfather asked, "does the telephone ring when I dial his number?"

I thought of a couple bright remarks, but under the circumstances I didn't dare.

"One would think," Grandfather said, "that when a man dies the telephone company would have enough sense to disconnect his telephone."

"He probably had a wife," I said, "and she'd want to keep the telephone, wouldn't she?"

Grandfather snapped his fingers. "Children. If he isn't living, his children inherit Professor Pesman's money. I think we'd better call on Mrs. Vaughan."

Grandfather sent me over to a filling station to ask for a map of Windalia. They didn't have one, and the attendant looked at me as if I'd just asked him to spell my name for me. I went back to the car, and in the meantime Grandfather had noticed that the Vaughan address was First Street, and we were parked on First Street. I drove two blocks and found the number, an apartment building.

We went up to the door and rang the bell under the name, "Vaughan." There was no response.

"We're wasting our time," Grandfather said. "If she's not there to answer the telephone, she isn't there to come to the door."

A woman came up the walk with a bag of groceries. We stepped back out of her way, and she opened the door with a key. "Were you looking for someone?" she asked.

"We were looking for information about Professor Vaughan," Grandfather said.

"He's gone for the summer," she said. And then, before either of us could get his mouth closed, she stepped inside and the door slammed shut behind her.

We sat in the car for awhile, neither of us saying anything. "I'm going to get to the bottom of this," Grandfather announced finally, "if I have to spend the summer here."

"I've heard Sheriff Pilkins say that being dead is a pretty good alibi," I said. "Do you suppose—"

"No," Grandfather said, "I don't."

"Well, either Professor Vaughan pretended to be dead and went away for the summer, or he died and pretended to go away for the summer. You can't have it both ways."

"I don't want it either way," Grandfather said. "Let's go back to that Administrative Building."

"Supposing that woman was Mrs. Vaughan," I said, "and she won't believe her husband is dead. I've heard of cases like that."

"Johnny," Grandfather said, "I take back what I said about voting for you for sheriff. You're as bad as Pilkins. Now take me to the Administration

Building."

We had to start over again with the girl in the lobby, but this time Grandfather's request was very much to the point. He wanted to see the president. The girl seemed pretty sure that the president didn't want to see him. We probably did look a little less dignified than we would have liked. We had on our Sunday clothes, but then we'd had them on during the trip the day before, and by that time they had a kind of Monday look about them.

Again the girl passed us along to a higher administrative level, but this time it was a different level, a middle-aged woman who was certain that I was a potential student for Landsdorf College, and it was really the admissions officer that we wanted to see. Grandfather held out for the president. She still sent us down the hall to another office, and the woman there sent us to still another office, and finally we met a third woman, who turned out to be the president's secretary. The closer we got to the president, the younger and prettier the woman was, which proved to me that even a college president can be sensitive to his surroundings.

Grandfather explained to the secretary that he had been talking with the president that morning, and that he needed further information. The secretary plainly didn't believe a word of it, but she took Grandfather's name, and told a little box on her desk that a Mr. Rastin wanted to see him, and the box told her to send Mr. Rastin in.

The president wasn't one of those absent-minded professors. He remembered us right away, though of course he'd only been talking with us an hour before, and I suppose even an absent-minded professor wouldn't be that absent-minded.

Grandfather helped himself to a chair, and folded his hands, and asked the president if he'd ever heard of a Charles Pesman. The president hadn't.

"Charlie Pesman was a friend of mine," Grandfather said. "He died last week, and Professor Andrew Vaughan is his principal heir."

"Ah!" the president said. "But as I told you, Andy Vaughan died last spring. Is the estate large?"

"I'd call it large," Grandfather said. "They haven't got it all added up yet, but they think it will amount to close to a half million dollars."

The president gave out with a very unpresidential whistle. "How unfortunate," he said. "Andy could have endowed that scholarship fund that interested him so, and also made a substantial contribution towards our new English building. I'd say your friend timed his death very badly."

"It wasn't exactly his doing," Grandfather said. "He was murdered."

The president was still smiling at the joke he thought he'd made, but his face straightened out in a hurry. "Indeed," he said. "But I'm afraid I can't be of any help to you. Andy died before your friend died, so of course he can't inherit anything. It sounds to me as if you have a splendid opportunity for an unlimited number of lawyers."

"The will specifies," Grandfather said, "that if Andrew Vaughan is dead, the estate shall go to his children. I'd like to know if he had any children."

"As a matter of fact, he did," the president said. "He had one or two daughters—I don't recall which—but she or they died in infancy. His son George—a splendid young man, and one of our students—died in World War II. He was awarded the Distinguished Service Cross, posthumously, of course. Mrs. Vaughan was very broken up over it and she died not long afterwards. And then there was a second son, Mark."

"When did he die?" Grandfather asked dryly.

"Oh, but he didn't. Mark is a brilliant young man, and currently an instructor in our history department. Then Mark will inherit—"

"As I understand it, he will. I'd like to talk with him."

"I can't say offhand whether he's teaching this summer. Just a moment, please."

He got out the same list of names we'd already seen twice, and checked it over. "No," he said. "He isn't teaching this summer. He may be doing research somewhere. I understand that he has a book in progress."

"Did he live with his father?" Grandfather asked.

"I believe he did."

"That explains a lot of things. We just called at that address, and a woman told us Professor Vaughan was gone for the summer. Probably she meant the son."

"Undoubtedly," the president said with a grin. "He is not a professor, but I have no doubt that he will be, some day, and to the layman all college teachers are professors. I'm very happy for Mark. I'm sure he's the kind of young man who will use his inheritance wisely." He sounded as if he were ready to order blueprints for that new English building.

"Have you any idea how I could get in touch with him?" Grandfather asked.

"I could ask my secretary to check, and see if he left a forwarding address."

"I'd appreciate that," Grandfather said. "One thing more. Do you happen to have a picture of Mark Vaughan?"

"Certainly."

The president went over to a book shelf, of which there were many, and took down a book. It *was* a yearbook—it had *1963* in large numbers on the front—so Grandfather's idea was better than he'd realized. The president leafed through it until he found the page he wanted, and passed it across to Grandfather. Grandfather nodded and passed it back.

"Thank you," he said. "If you'll ask your secretary about the forwarding address, we won't take any more of your time."

We took considerable amount of the secretary's time, but finally she scribbled on a memo pad and hung up the telephone. She gave the paper to Grandfather, and he thanked her, and headed for the door.

It was all I could do to keep up with him. He left the building and galloped across the street to a drugstore, getting grazed by two cars and causing consternation in the traffic on First Street. He dove into a telephone booth and a moment later I heard him spelling Wiston for the operator. When he came out he pocketed the piece of paper, and said, "All right. Now we can go home."

"Which salesman was it?"

"The first one," he said. "The young fellow with the briefcase. That was Mark Vaughan." He grinned happily, and patted me on the back. "This trip was a fine idea. I'm glad I thought of it."

CHAPTER VII

The address that Mark Vaughan had given the college—for emergency purposes only, the president's secretary said, and Grandfather told me later that if ever there was an emergency this was it—was in care of general delivery in Benton Harbor, Michigan.

Now Sheriff Pilkins may have his little peculiarities, but give him a *bona fide*, Grade A lead like this one and he usually doesn't waste any time in getting after it. Even so he displayed an unusual efficiency in catching Mark Vaughan, though as Grandfather pointed out afterwards, the Benton Harbor and State Police did all the work. Vaughan was arrested Tuesday morning, and Sheriff Pilkins telephoned right away to tell Grandfather about it, and to invite him to a session he was going to hold the first thing that afternoon at the Courthouse.

"What's the idea?" I asked Grandfather.

"The idea is to return Vaughan to the scene of the crime, and make him confess, or something."

"There's nothing wrong with that," I said. "I imagine it'll save everyone a lot of trouble if he confesses."

"If he has anything to confess, it will."

"Don't you think he did it?"

"In this country," Grandfather said, "a man is supposed to be presumed to be innocent until proven guilty. Most police officers work it the other way around. In a sense they have to, because they wouldn't catch any criminals if they went around presuming that everyone was innocent, but they could handle it a lot differently than they do. Take this case. If I was in charge of things, I'd tell Vaughn he was an important witness because he found the body—which is true—and I'd get his story and ask him to keep in touch with me. Then I'd back off and keep an eye on him while I thought the whole thing over. Pilkins has grabbed him on a charge of murder, so he'll be hauled back here under arrest. If he's guilty this doesn't accomplish anything except to get his guard up and keep it there, and if he's innocent it's a terrible thing."

I said the man hadn't acted very innocent, running off and hiding the way he did, and Grandfather said we hadn't seen him leave, so we weren't in a position to say whether he ran or not, and it wasn't right to say he hid when he was traveling around in a perfectly respectable job using his own name.

The situation seemed funny to me, and I started to laugh.

"What's the matter?" Grandfather asked.

"The sheriff is going to hate you. First you find a suspect for him, actually the first good one he's had, and now you're going to go over there and try to convince him that the man's innocent."

"No one is going to convince Pilkins that this man is innocent," Grandfather said. "Whether Vaughan did it or not, he's in trouble."

We were at the Courthouse at one o'clock. Mrs. Glover seemed to be mildly excited over the prospect of seeing a real live murderer, but the others had other things on their minds. Mr. Boyd was still irked because Junior Temple wouldn't tell them whether they should move out or not and he said he was leaving at the end of the month regardless of what happened. Pete Kruger had started to worry about what would happen to the laboratory animals and he wasn't caring whether the sheriff had caught the murderer or not. Willie was saying nothing, as usual.

Then the sheriff arrived, with three deputies and Mark Vaughan. Steve Carling had Vaughan handcuffed—Steve likes to use handcuffs, and I've heard the he even makes his wife wear a pair around the house, though I don't know if it's true. Ed Fellows and Sam Baker came about the same time and the sheriff brought everyone into the big living room and cleared the deck for action.

"Ed," he said, "ever see this man before?"

"Sure," Ed said. "That's the salesman I told you about."

"How about you, Sam?"

"That's the guy," Sam said.

Vaughan spoke for the first time. "Is this really necessary? I'm not denying that I was here that day."

The sheriff told him to speak when spoken to, and asked Grandfather and me if we could identify him. Grandfather could, and it certainly wasn't any problem for me. He was wearing the same suit—the same necktie, even—and he looked just about as upset as he had before, though this time he wasn't sweating over it.

The sheriff told Ed and Sam that they could leave. They did, though Sam hinted that he wasn't pressed for time, and Ed for once wasn't worrying about his cows.

Then the sheriff started in on the others. "Mrs. Glover, have you seen this man before?"

She said no, with a coy smile that suggested maybe she wished she had. The sheriff saw the smile, and scowled. "How about you, Boyd?"

"If I've seen him anywhere, I don't remember it," Mr. Boyd said.

"Pete?"

Pete's mind was elsewhere and he had to be asked twice. He said no. "Willie?"

Willie was sitting in his usual place on the floor in the corner. He got up and walked over to Vaughan and stood there for a moment, looking him over good. Then he turned to the sheriff and shook his head, and went back to the corner.

"That's all for you, then," the sheriff said. Mrs. Glover and Mr. Boyd and Pete left the room. Willie stayed in the corner, and the sheriff didn't seem to care, or maybe he didn't notice. Willie was always easy to overlook.

"I haven't talked to him yet," the sheriff said to Grandfather. "I thought you'd want to hear it, since you found him."

"I didn't find him," Grandfather said. "I just identified him. But go ahead."

"Just to begin with, he claims he didn't know the professor was dead. That ought to be worth an explanation. How about it, Vaughan?"

"I already explained to the officer who arrested me," Vaughan said, being very patient with the sheriff. "Didn't he tell you?"

"He did, but I didn't believe it. I'd like to hear if from you."

"I'm a college teacher," Vaughan said, "and I took a job this summer selling encyclopedias, in the hope of making a little money. This is something I find difficult to do in my regular profession."

"Excuse me," the sheriff said, "but I was under the impression that college teachers got paid."

"You were under the wrong impression. The starting salary for an instructor at Landsdorf College is three thousand, six hundred and forty dollars for nine months. I'm trying to get a book written, and it's costing me money. There aren't any source materials in Windalia, so I have to go where they are, or order copies. Either way it's expensive. Also, my father died in April after a long illness, and left a pile of medical bills. I ended the school year in debt, so I had to take this summer job."

"None of which explains why you didn't know Professor Pesman was dead. Are you boycotting the radio and the newspapers?"

"You might say that I am. Any free time I have, I work on my book."

"What's the book about?" Grandfather asked.

"It's a history of the Populist Party. My specialty is American History."

The sheriff said to Grandfather, with exaggerated politeness, "Have you any more irrelevant questions, Mr. Rastin?"

"It isn't always possible to tell whether a question is relevant or not until it's been asked," Grandfather said.

"You should know," the sheriff said. He rubbed his hands together, and said slyly, "Now, then, Mr. Vaughan. You say you're in financial difficulties."

"I have that impression," Vaughan said.

"But it's nothing that half a million dollars wouldn't cure—if you were to inherit it, say."

Vaughan smiled. "That would take care of the situation nicely. Unfortunately, few of my relatives have any money, and those who do wouldn't be leaving it to me."

The sheriff exchanged glances with Grandfather, and came off second best. "Supposing you tell us what happened when you called on the professor last week," he said to Vaughan."

"Supposing I go back a bit further, and tell you why I called on the professor last week," Vaughan said.

"Suit yourself."

"As I said, my father died in April. He had one death-bed request. When he was a young man, he'd invested a substantial amount of money in a corporation set up by a friend of his. The corporation went bankrupt, but father thought the friend might still be working on some of the ideas the corporation was supposed to develop, and that it was just possible that something might come of them. If anything did, Father wanted me to use the money to establish a scholarship fund in his name."

"How much money was he expecting?" the sheriff asked.

"I think he hoped to get his investment back, and if he remembered correctly that was thirty thousand dollars. The friend was Charles Pesman, and father told me he was living somewhere near Wiston, Michigan. He asked me not to write to him, or see him, or anything like that. I gathered that Mr. Pesman took his time about honoring his obligations, and didn't care to be rushed. Father implied that if I bothered him at all, there likely wouldn't be any money forthcoming."

"Do you know the name of that corporation?" Grandfather asked.

"The Modern Merchandising Corporation. Father still had his stock certificates and I saved them—though I don't know why. This Pesman struck me as an interesting person, because as near as I could make out from what Father told me, he had been working on some kind of a subliminal advertising scheme back in the 1920's. I thought that a man who'd been thirty years ahead of his time might be worth knowing."

"But the corporation went broke," Grandfather said.

"As Father remembered it, research ate up all the available money and Pesman couldn't raise any more. End of corporation."

"What all this adds up to," the sheriff said, "is that your father told you to stay away from Pesman, so you went to see him."

"Well, naturally I was curious about him. You see, he was the ogre of my childhood. Mother didn't share Father's optimism about Pesman, and when Father wasn't around she told all kinds of stories about the horrible man who'd devoured our family security. She never mentioned his name, and when I was a kid I half thought she was making it up. When I finally learned the truth I was—curious. Anyway, I took this summer job with Forest and Everhard. They have a very good encyclopedia, and their sales manager convinced me that I could make a good income out of it, and he was right. I've been doing very well. My territory covers a number of small towns in south-west Michigan, and since on my way there I passed close to Wiston I thought I owed it to myself to look up the family ogre."

"How does that square with you're being too busy to read a newspaper?" the sheriff asked.

"I thought the family ogre was worth making an exception. I had no intention of letting Pesman know who I was, of course. I thought I'd just look around and see what sort of person he was. So I stopped by here on a Saturday, and drifted around Wiston and that little town—"

"Borgville," Grandfather growled.

"Something like that, hoping to pick up some information about Pesman, but I didn't get a thing out of it. I couldn't even get a good look at his house, either from the highway or that back road, but those signs by the highway intrigued me. It seemed to me that I had a legitimate excuse for calling on him because I was a salesman. The first chance I had, which was Tuesday, I came back to give it a try. You know what happened then."

Sheriff Pilkins made a sound that came out midway between a laugh and a snarl. "Sure. We know what happened then. But we'd like to have you tell us about it."

"Well, through that hedge you come to a short path, and then at the end of the path you have a choice, left or right. I turned left, and then had another choice, and then there were several choices, and so on. I was some distance into the thing before I finally realized what it was, and it seemed to me that Pesman was having one more laugh on our family. That thought made me just mad enough to try to keep going. I don't know how long I was in there, because I hadn't thought to look at my watch when I started, but eventually I rounded a corner and all but stumbled over a man's body. He was lying face down, and his head had been smashed. I checked, and couldn't find any pulse, and considering what had happened to his head that was probably a silly thing to do. Then I wanted to get out of there fast and get help, but by that time I'd lost all sense of direction and hadn't the faintest idea of how to go about it. I still don't know how I made it, but I did, and there was a mob of people and a police officer waiting by the road. I thought, 'Ah—they already know about it,' and I told the officer I'd found a dead man, and they all started laughing. It was the darndest experience I've ever had."

"You went back into the maze again," the sheriff said.

"But not far," Vaughan said. "When I started I was mad enough at Pesman to tear right through that maze and spit in his face, but the feeling didn't last much beyond the first turn. I went to the right, the second time, and if anything it was more confusing than the other way had been. It didn't take long for me to decide that Father had been right, and Charles Pesman was best left unmolested. I probably wasn't in there ten minutes the second time. Everyone was gone when I came out, and I got into my car and headed west for a little town called Alcanna, which was the next place on my schedule. End of story."

I chanced to glance over at Willie, who was still sitting cross-legged in the corner. His large eyes were intent on Vaughan's face. I'd never seen him concentrate so on anything, unless maybe a game of checkers. I'd have given something to know what he was thinking about.

"Any questions?" the sheriff asked Grandfather.

"I can't think of any," Grandfather said. "It was a very complete story."

"It seemed to me that a pertinent detail or two was missing," the sheriff said.

"Am I allowed to ask a question?" Vaughan said.

"I suppose so."

"Why did you arrest me? I'd have come back, if they'd just told me you wanted me."

"I arrested you," the sheriff said, "for the murder of Charles Pesman. You'll probably be arraigned tomorrow morning."

Vaughan gave him the blankest look I've ever seen on a man's face. "Why the devil would I want to kill Pesman?"

"I was hoping you'd tell me that," the sheriff said.

Vaughan looked about the room—at the deputies, at Grandfather, at me, at Willie. "I want a lawyer," he said finally.

"You'll get one," the sheriff said.

Vaughan turned to Grandfather. "You have an honest face, which is more than I can say for some of the others present. Will you send me the best lawyer in town?"

Grandfather nodded.

"What a crazy idea!" Vaughan said. "The only interest I had in the man was to find out if he would restore the family fortune, and he certainly can't do that when he's dead."

"Take him outside," the sheriff said, "and see if he'll show you what happened."

The deputies went away with him, and then one of them came back to say that Vaughan wasn't showing anything, or talking any more, until he had seen a lawyer.

"Take him back to town, then," the sheriff said. "I'll be along later."

"So he doesn't know he's the heir," Grandfather said.

"He isn't letting on that he knows. I figure there's no point in my mentioning it."

"I suppose not," Grandfather said. "If he already knows, you wouldn't be telling him anything. If he really doesn't know, then you'd have to get to work rigging up another motive for him, and that might be a lot of trouble."

The sheriff's face shifted to stage two, which was a moderate shade of pink. Grandfather spoke again before he could answer. "I wonder what happened to the letter that Temple wrote."

"We've traced it," the sheriff said. "It was sent in care of Landsdorf College, and someone in the college mail room figured it might be intended for Andrew Vaughan's son and sent it to the history department, and someone there stuck it in Mark Vaughan's office mail box. It was still there this morning, and it's being sent back unopened. What lawyer are you going to get for him?"

"Norm Temple," Grandfather said. "Who else? Vaughan is a fine-looking young fellow, isn't he?"

"He's just about the best-looking murderer I've ever seen," the sheriff said.

The sheriff left, and Willie scooted off somewhere, and Grandfather and I were alone.

"Do *you* think he did it?" I asked Grandfather.

"I don't know," Grandfather said. "I'd feel much better about all this if I had some answers to a few pertinent questions. Such as—what was the professor doing down in the maze that afternoon? And—did Vaughan know that the professor was in the maze? And—if he did know it, how did he happen to find him there? And—if he didn't know it, and happened on him by accident, was it also an accident that he happened to have a piece of pipe in his briefcase? Either way we have a staggering series of coincidences, or there's some very simple explanation that no one's hit upon. I don't like coincidences, and if the sheriff can't come up with that simple explanation, I'm going to think he's arrested the wrong man. Now let's go to Wiston. I want to see how Bob is getting on with the painting."

We found Bob Meyers in a foul mood. He had the living room ceiling finished, and he was grumbling about this new-fangled notion Grandfather had of having the ceilings a lighter color than the walls and different colors in every room in the house. Not only did it create a problem in buying paint, but it made a nasty problem in painting where two colors came together, and he was just about of a mind to chuck the whole business.

"Why don't you use masking tape?" Grandfather asked.

"What's that?" Bob wanted to know.

"You did a real nice job on the ceiling," Grandfather said.

That thawed Bob a little, but he went on grumbling between brush strokes, about all those colors being a waste of time, and how the different shades would all look the same when they got a layer of good, honest dirt on them. We started to leave, and he added, kind of an afterthought, "Say, your plumbing is stopped up."

And it certainly was.

Grandfather called a plumber, and after some fussing around the plumber told him that roots from the poplar tree in the front yard had gotten into the pipe leading out to the street. Grandfather didn't want to believe it. He said it had never happened before, and the plumber said, well, the tree was never that big before, either, which was not a point Grandfather could argue very well, though he tried. It turned out that this plumber was not equipped to take roots out of a pipe, which meant Grandfather had to call someone else, which meant two plumbing bills. When we left the house he was as disgusted as a man can be.

Up town there were parking problems which, as Grandfather pointed out several times while we were driving around looking, were just one more reason why there should be a law against large towns. I said they might also be a reason for a law against automobiles, and Grandfather agreed. What with the mood he was in after dealing with the plumbers, he was also willing to rule out airplanes, railroad trains and indoor plumbing while he was at it. "The two things that ruined American character," he said, "were letting women vote, and moving the plumbing inside the house."

I told him this was getting too far off the subject of parking, and would he mind watching for a place. We found one, a good six blocks from the Temple law offices, and Grandfather grumbled all the way over there.

Along the way we met Jerry Krohl coming out of the branch office of Strobel, Ross, Beal and Larkins. Krohl shook hands with both of us—I guess he thought I might grow up to be an investor—and told Grandfather it was a fine day, which Grandfather doubted, and asked him if he'd heard that Sheriff Pilkins had arrested Professor Pesman's murderer.

"Seems to me I did hear a rumor to that effect," Grandfather said.

Krohl said it was good news, mentioned the weather again, tossed in a remark on the foreign situation, and—all in the same sentence—asked Grandfather whether he owned any stocks.

"Most of my money is in real estate," Grandfather said.

"Real estate can be a fine investment," Krohl said. "Of course, there are problems of upkeep."

"There sure are," Grandfather said bitterly.

"Not to mention taxes, and the difficulty of finding desirable tenants. It seems to me that owning real estate might sometimes be a nuisance."

"It is most of the time," Grandfather said.

"I'd be happy to tell you about the advantages of owning stock. I think a utilities stock, such as Western Power and Light, would be an excellent investment for you. It pays a good dividend, and it's a growth situation."

"Perhaps some other time," Grandfather said.

"Why don't I mail you some information about it?"

"Do that," Grandfather said.

Krohl made a note in his pocket secretary, shook hands with both of us again, and hurried away tossing a final remark over his shoulder. Something about the weather.

We had a short conference with Temple and Temple in that big office of theirs. Grandfather told them that he'd located the professor's heir, but there was a mild complication because the sheriff had just arrested him for murder. He'd be needing a lawyer.

Old Man Temple considered the matter, wondering out loud if there would be any conflict of interest involved if he represented the heir in a murder trial, since he'd been the professor's lawyer, and Junior was the executor of the professor's estate.

Grandfather said that he was no expert in legal ethics—he even implied that he hadn't known there were any—but he figured that if the heir was guilty there could be all kinds of conflicts and complications, whereas if the heir was innocent it would be the duty of the professor's lawyer and the executor of his estate to get him off so the estate could be turned over to him.

Old Man Temple thought that was funny and he relaxed, and said he'd go over and talk with Mark Vaughan.

"Speaking of the estate," Grandfather said, "did you let Krohl sell that stock?"

"What stock was that?" Junior Temple wanted to know.

"Good Heavens!" Grandfather said. "Last week the man was practically tearing his hair because some fool stock the professor bought was falling straight through to China and had to be sold immediately. You mean he didn't even tell you about it?"

"Oh," Old Man Temple said. "Was that what he wanted? He telephoned and said he wanted to talk to us about the professor's stocks, but I thought he was just looking for an opening to sell me some stocks."

"Well, you'd better see him," Grandfather said. "From the way he was carrying on, I got the impression that if this stock isn't sold there won't be any estate."

Old Man Temple told Junior to give Krohl a call and find out what was bothering him. "Not that we can do anything about it," he said to Grandfather. "We can't do a thing until we have letters of administration from the probate court, and it'll be another two weeks before we get them."

"That seems like a shame," Grandfather said. "If Krohl is right—"

"He's probably right. He's a good man, and the professor did very well dealing with him. Be we can't authorize him to do a thing until we receive the letter of administration."

He got his hat and headed for the county jail to see Mark Vaughan, and Grandfather and I started the six-block walk back to my jalopy.

"I don't understand why they won't let Mr. Krohl sell the stock," I said.

"I don't either," Grandfather said. "Or maybe I do. The law has certain procedures that have to be followed, and it isn't going to hurry them up just on account of what's happening on the stock market. Temple probably means that Junior won't be the executor officially until the court appoints him and it'll be a couple more weeks before the court gets around to that. It all sounds to me like a real good reason for staying out of the stock market. I've never made a penny out of stocks, but I've never lost a penny either, and I'm satisfied to leave it that way."

CHAPTER VIII

The next morning some pamphlets and things arrived from Strobel, Ross, Beal and Larkins, along with a letter from Mr. Krohl saying this was the material he'd promised to send, and he hoped he could be of service.

Grandfather pigeonholed the whole package, but I dug it out and went through it. There was a little book explaining how the New York Stock Exchange operated, which I thought interesting enough to save for school. There was also a pamphlet about something called Mutual Funds, which I didn't exactly understand, and some information about some corporations Mr. Krohl thought Grandfather ought to buy stock in.

I read some of these twice. The first time through every one of them looked like the opportunity of a lifetime, and the second time I began to pick out phrases that began, "providing that," or "assuming that," or "on the basis of," and ended up wondering if the companies might go broke the next day.

Later in the morning it started to rain, and Bob Meyers called Grandfather not long after that to tell him that the roof was leaking. We tore over to Wiston, where we found that something had rusted away around the chimney, and Grandfather had to hop to it and locate a roofing man who didn't mind working in the rain, so the upstairs ceilings wouldn't get ruined. Grandfather didn't say anything at all, but it looked to me as if the prospects were bright for Jerry Krohl to sell some stock.

Fortunately the rain didn't last long, and I told Grandfather I could think of more interesting things to do than watch someone repair a roof, so I drove up town to kill time until lunch.

First I picked up a copy of the previous day's paper, to see what it had to say about the murder. There was an article about Mark Vaughan, and it pointed out, among other things, that it had only taken Sheriff Pilkins a week to unravel an exceptionally complicated murder case and make an arrest.

I spent some time wandering around in the dime store, wondering if Grandfather had been pulling my leg when he told me that once you could actually buy things there for a dime. Then I went over to the library and read a magazine until it was time to go after Grandfather.

On the way back to my jalopy I met Old Man Temple, who was on his way to lunch. I asked him how he was getting along with his new client. He said that he'd broken the news to Vaughan about him being the heir to most of the professor's money. At first Vaughan wouldn't believe it, and then when Temple convinced him it was the truth he threw up his hands and said he wouldn't need a lawyer after all, that with a motive like that the sheriff could prove he did it even if he'd been in Bangkok on the day it happened. I asked Mr. Temple where Bangkok was, and he didn't know.

"Vaughan's preliminary hearing will be Monday morning," Mr. Temple said. "Tell your Grandfather not to miss it. Matter of fact, I might even use him as a witness. I know how he likes to testify in court."

I told him Grandfather would appreciate that.

"Ted Frazier is the Justice," he said. "Monday at ten o'clock. It'll be the most startling preliminary hearing Borg County has ever had."

"How come it's so soon?" I asked. "I thought it took months to get ready for a murder trial."

"It isn't a trial, it's a preliminary hearing. Even so, our esteemed County Attorney screamed murder about it coming so soon, but Ted Frazier is a friend of mine, and I've done him one or two favors, so I managed to get it set for Monday. I don't want Vaughan in jail any longer than absolutely necessary."

I told him he sounded mighty confident, and he winked at me, and told me not to miss that hearing.

A block further on I met Mr. Boyd, and he said that he and Mrs. Glover and Pete Kruger were moving out that afternoon, but Willie was staying on as a kind of caretaker. I asked him what would happen to the laboratory animals, because there was a guinea pig there I wouldn't have minded having myself, and he said he didn't know but he supposed Willie would look after them until someone decided what to do with them. "Unless Junior Temple is the one that will have to decide," he said. "In that case the animals will be there until they all die of old age."

What with these delays I was already late when I got back to my jalopy, and there I found, right smack in the middle of my windshield under the wiper, a parking ticket.

This is another point I knew Grandfather would make about big towns if I told him about the ticket, which naturally I had no intention of doing. In Borgville we make strangers feel welcome. I want you to know that in Borgville you can park anywhere you want, for as long as you want, and if your car isn't actually obstructing traffic or damaging someone's lawn, no one will say anything. If it is, someone will politely ask you to move it. In Borgville a person from out-of-town is a guest, and tickets are something we sell to the annual Volunteer Fire Department Ice Cream Social, if you happen to be around at that time of the year. You can even park your car by a fire hydrant, if you feel like it, because Borgville is a modern town with more than one fire hydrant, and if your car is blocking one the firemen will use another one.

But in a big town—well, take Wiston. The sign said sixty-minute parking and I'd only been there a little over an hour and a half, and there already was a parking ticket.

The ticket said the fine was one dollar, but there was a reduced rate of twenty-five cents if it was paid within an hour of the offense. I drove over to the city hall, and found a parking place, and got inside with my quarter just under the wire. A man in police uniform took my money and wrote out a receipt, and when he thanked me I didn't tell him he was welcome.

By that time I was in a panic to get back to pick up Grandfather because I was nearly an hour late and I didn't have to wonder what it was he would say to me. I'd heard it once or twice before. I left the city hall at a gallop, and nearly bowled over a little man who chanced to be walking by at that moment. I excused myself, and he said quite all right, and then I stood staring after him for a full twenty seconds before I turned my back on my jalopy and followed him.

It was the dried-up little salesman who'd been lost in the maze the night of the professor's murder.

He wasn't in much of a hurry. He walked along slowly, stopping now and then to look into a store window, and finally he turned in at a restaurant. I watched through the window while he had a long conversation with the waitress, and then he lit his pipe and settled back to wait for his food, and I went across the street to a drugstore, and found a seat at the fountain where I could look over at the restaurant, and ordered a root beer and a hot dog.

I knew the smart thing for me to do would have been to call the sheriff right then, but the phone booth was at the back of the store, and I was afraid the salesman might get away while I was telephoning. So I sat there for nearly forty minutes, and had two more root beers and a second hot dog, and finally I saw him leave. I swallowed the last of my root beer and took out after him.

It was probably the shortest tailing job on record. He turned the corner by the restaurant, got into a car, and drove away.

I was close enough to get the license number, but I had nothing to write with and nothing to write on. I stood there on the corner with my eyes closed, mumbling the number over and over until I was sure I had it memorized, and then I stopped a woman and told her it was an emergency, and she gave me an old envelope to write on, and loaned me a ball point pen. I wrote down the license number and the make of the car, and returned the pen with a thanks. Then I ran all the way back to the city hall where I'd left my jalopy.

Darned if I didn't have another parking ticket.

When I finally reached the house Grandfather was sitting on the steps waiting for me. He bellowed, "Johnny!" before I got the door opened, and then when I walked up to him he didn't say anything at all. The moral is—if you have to be late, be real late. One hour, and he'd have blistered me. Two hours and a half, and he was too mad to speak.

"Come on," I said. "I have to see the sheriff right away."

"Who did you run into?" he asked.

He walked all around the car, and assured himself that there weren't any dents or scratches that hadn't been there before, and then he got in and I drove over to the County Building.

Sheriff Pilkins wasn't in, but he came in while I was asking about him. He took the two of us into his private office, and sat down behind his desk, and let us find our own chairs. "What is it?" he asked Grandfather.

"Ask Johnny," Grandfather said. "I just came along for the ride."

"Really?" the sheriff said. "Are you in trouble, Johnny?"

"I don't think so," I said. "I have important information for you, but I incurred some expenses in getting it. If you want the information, you'll have to reimburse me."

The sheriff looked quickly at Grandfather, and when he'd convinced himself that Grandfather knew nothing about it, he turned back to me. "What sort of expenses?"

"I'll break it down for you," I said. "Two parking tickets at twenty-five cents each. Two hot dogs at twenty cents each. Three root beers at ten cents each. Total of a dollar and twenty cents, plus two cents sales tax. That makes it a dollar twenty-two."

"You're really a reckless spender when you're after information," the sheriff said. "You weren't using those root beers to bribe anyone, were you?"

"No sir," I said. "They were part of my disguise."

The sheriff thought this over, and then he took a dollar bill from his wallet, and fished a quarter from his side pocket. "I'm feeling reckless to-day," he said. "Here—keep the change."

"No sir," I said. "I'm not one of those characters who take payola and pads expense accounts. All I want is the money I'm honestly entitled to."

I gave him his three cents change, and he spun the pennies around on his desk and nodded. "What's the information?"

"I've found the missing salesman," I said. "He's driving a '61 Ford with an Ohio license plate. Here."

"I'll have him picked up," the sheriff said. He took my borrowed envelope with the license number and sent out to give the order. Then he came back, and tilted back in his chair, and said, "Tell me how it happened."

So I told him about getting the parking ticket, and going over to city hall to pay for it, and running into the salesman on the way out and following him.

He heard me out to the end, where I'd gotten the second ticket, and then he said, "Johnny, there's one thing that I don't understand. You charged me for two parking tickets. The way I see it, it was only the second one that you got while you were working for me. The first one you got on your own. Why did you make me pay for that one too?"

"If I hadn't gotten that one, I wouldn't have gone over to the city hall to pay for it, and then I wouldn't have run into the salesman on the way out and maybe you'd never have found him."

"There's a flaw in that reasoning somewhere," the sheriff said, "but I'm darned if I know where it is. Did anyone ever tell you that you take after your Grandfather?"

"His grandfather has never been two hours and a half late for an appointment," Grandfather said. "But I guess I'll have to overlook it, seeing as how he was working for you. I'm not sure, though, but what I shouldn't charge you for my lunch, which I haven't had yet."

"And which you're going to miss altogether if you wait for me to pay for it," the sheriff said.

His telephone rang. He answered it and said, "Good. I'll send over for him."

He hung up, and tilted back again. "That was the city police," he said. "They have our salesman."

"Wow!" I said. "How'd they happen to get him so fast?"

"He was over at city hall when the call came in—paying for a parking ticket."

If being arrested made this salesman nervous, he wasn't showing it when they brought him in. The expression on his face reminded me a little of the one Grandfather had been wearing when I showed up two hours and a half late. He stood in front of the sheriff's desk, and ignored the chair the sheriff pointed at, and asked, "What's the meaning of this?"

Someone had given the sheriff another cigar, and he got it out, and tried both ends for size, and lit it. He blew a cloud of smoke into the salesman's face. "Haven't we met somewhere before?" he asked.

"If we have I don't remember it, and if I did I wouldn't remember it with pleasure."

"Thanks," the sheriff said. He asked Grandfather, "Is this the guy?"

Grandfather nodded.

"I'd say so, too," the sheriff said. "Though I wasn't paying as much attention to him that night as I should have been. Who else saw him? Boyd? Willie? Mrs. Glover would make the best witness. She fed him. I'll send someone out to the Courthouse after her."

"She may not be there," I said. "She's moving to town this afternoon."

"Johnny, you're a regular bureau of information," the sheriff said. "If I was sure you wouldn't grow up to be a Democrat, like your grandfather, I'd have a job waiting for you when you get through high school." He picked up the telephone.

"Never mind," the salesman said. "If you're referring to my fiasco with Pesman's maze, you don't need witnesses. I'm not denying I was there. Why should I? I don't remember seeing you, though."

"My fault, for not introducing myself properly," the sheriff said. "It seems to me that you were a wee bit negligent on that score yourself. Your name?"

"James Collins."

"Occupation?"

"I am an Associate Professor of Physics at Southern Ohio University."

The sheriff stopped writing. All three of us stared at Collins, and he kept his eyes on the sheriff, as if daring him to make something of it.

"Why were you masquerading as a salesman?" the sheriff asked.

"I wasn't," Collins said. "Whatever gave you that idea?"

Sheriff Pilkins took time to inspect his cigar. "Now that I think of it, what did give us that idea?"

"As soon as we found out that someone was lost in the maze, we took it for granted that it was a salesman, the one who'd been there that afternoon. When this gentleman was brought in we all assumed that he was another salesman, and I don't think anyone bothered to ask him."

"Right," the sheriff said. "Because it usually was a salesman in the maze, on account of the signs. By the way, Rastin, have you noticed that the signs have been taken down, and a gate put in the hedge? I gave Junior Temple an ultimatum. He said he had no authority, but I noticed that he got the job done anyway. Where were we? So you are Professor Collins, and not a salesman. Would you mind telling us why you went into the maze?"

"Yes," Collins said, "since I don't enjoy making a fool of myself I suppose I have no choice. I have been offered an appointment as Professor of Physics at Wiston College. I came here to see what the school was like, and to talk with Dean Morris. I was staying with an old friend, Bill Alford, of the Psychology Department, and he told me about Pesman's maze. I was curious to give it a try. Bill told me that Pesman would be pleased if I found my way through it, but he would also be pleased if I didn't, so I saw no harm in the project."

"No," the sheriff said. "It makes about as much sense as a lot of the things that have been going on around here. Your conduct after you were rescued was a little curious, though. Why did you run off?"

"In the first place, I was in a hurry. I am also considering appointments at two other schools, and I had promised to be in Pennsylvania early the next morning. I was disgusted with myself for getting lost in the maze and upsetting my travel plans. In the second place, the assembled gentlemen in the house obviously had more important matters than myself to concern themselves with. I felt that I had inconvenienced them enough as it was, and naturally I was highly embarrassed at getting myself into such a stupid predicament. It seemed best that I should quietly disappear. So I did."

Grandfather started to say something, but the sheriff flagged him down. "Just hold it a moment," he said. "I feel something coming here, and I don't like it. Just why do you think I had you picked up?"

"Why, I thought that Professor Pesman—" He turned and nodded in Grandfather's direction. "—had preferred charges of trespassing against me. I feel that this is unjust, under the circumstances, but I did trespass, and I suppose I am liable for whatever penalty or damages the law allows."

"Look here. Did you ever meet Professor Pesman before?"

"I haven't met him yet," Collins said with a smile. "I did see him that night, after I was rescued from the maze. I remember him perfectly well." He turned, and looked at Grandfather. "He has a striking profile."

"He thinks you're Pesman," the sheriff said. "Do you feel insulted?"

"Yes," Grandfather said. "But not for the reason you think."

"Good Lord, Collins! Do you mean to say *you* don't know Professor Pesman was murdered?"

"Murdered?" Collins looked Grandfather over very carefully. "Then you aren't Professor Pesman?"

"Since Professor Pesman is dead, and since I am, I hope, noticeably alive—"

"I see. That does alter things. No, I had no idea that Professor Pesman had been murdered."

"Don't tell me you're writing a book, too."

"As a matter of fact I am, a textbook on elementary physics. What does that have to do with it?"

"Nothing, I hope. How does it happen that you didn't hear about the murder?"

"Because I've been traveling, I suppose. I've been to Pennsylvania, and from there I drove back to Iowa, and now I'm here again. I've had conversations with the heads of two universities, I've examined facilities and studied curricula, and I've also given several lectures. It's been a rather busy week for me, and I don't believe I heard the word 'murder' mentioned."

"It's been mentioned a few times around here," the sheriff said. "It's been mentioned in the newspapers, and on radio and television, and I think I heard it once right here in this office. Well, tell me about last Tuesday."

Professor Collins didn't have much to tell. He'd been talking with Professor Alford about the maze, and he drove out to have a quick shot at it. He hadn't realized that the thing was so big, or he wouldn't have tried. He went in about four o'clock, and in no time at all he was absolutely lost. He kept trying to find his way out until it started to get dark, and then he sat down and yelled for help at regular intervals. Finally he heard a car stop, and someone shouted something at him. Nothing happened for a long time, and he kept yelling, and eventually someone came and led him out.

"What were you doing that day between one and two o'clock?"

"Let's see—that was a Tuesday. I believe I had lunch with Dean Morris that day, and if so we talked until one-thirty, at least. After that I had a conference with some of the physics faculty."

"How long do you expect to be in town?"

"Probably until the end of the week."

"And you say you're staying with Professor Alford?"

"Not this time. I felt that I imposed upon his hospitality excessively on my last stay. I'm at the Wiston Motel."

"All right. That'll be all—but get in touch with me before you leave town."

"Just a moment," Grandfather said. "How long have you taught at Southern Ohio University?"

"Too long," Professor Collins said. "Since 1927."

"Do you know a man named Andrew Vaughan?"

"Vaughan, Vaughan. What's his field?"

"English," Grandfather said.

"I believe I do vaguely remember him. Man with a beard, isn't he?"

"That I couldn't say."

"I believe there was an Andrew Vaughan at Southern many years ago. I couldn't tell you anything about him."

"One thing more. When did you arrive in Wiston?"

"Early this morning."

"I mean on your other visit."

"Oh. I arrived on Tuesday and left the following Tuesday—after I escaped from the maze. The dates were—I'd have to look at a calendar."

"The dates won't be necessary," Grandfather said. "Thank you."

The sheriff turned Professor Collins out, and then he laid down his cigar and glared at Grandfather. "What are you after now?"

"A murderer," Grandfather said. "Aren't you?"

"Collin couldn't have done it. He didn't get there until four o'clock, and anyway, I have the murderer."

Grandfather got up and stretched, and covered up a big yawn. "Of course you do," he said. "I keep forgetting that Vaughan has already been tried and found guilty. I might as well be going. Come along, Johnny."

"Now just a moment." The sheriff picked up his cigar, and made like a suction pump. "What about Collins?"

"The man's a liar. He certainly knew Professor Pesman, because Pesman taught at Southern Ohio University until 1935. I believe that if you check you'll find that Andrew Vaughan taught there too."

"Interesting. But he still couldn't have done the murder."

"Have you forgotten the mysterious stranger who hailed the professor on the street here in Wiston, and sent him hurrying home to lock his gate? Collins was in town that day."

The sheriff was puffing smoke like a steam locomotive. "Darn," he said. "Do you think he and Vaughan could have been in this together?"

"I'm only thinking that I'm very interested in this Professor Collins. Have you looked into the Modern Merchandising Corporation?"

"You mean that company of Pesman's that Vaughan's dad invested in? No, I haven't. Why?"

"It might be interesting to know who else lost money in that corporation."

"You mean—Collins?"

"Now wouldn't that be an amazing coincidence," Grandfather said. "Let's go, Johnny. I'd like to get some lunch before supper time."

CHAPTER IX

"You shouldn't have done that," I told Grandfather as we drove away. "The sheriff was in a chipper mood. He was making wise cracks, and he paid me a dollar twenty-two without batting an eye more than twice, and now you've made him go back to work again and ruined his whole day for him. Where do you want to eat?"

"Later," Grandfather said. "I want to talk with Junior Temple."

"It's after three-thirty. If you don't eat now, you'll spoil your supper."

"I guess I've had enough meals in my lifetime to be able to miss one," he said.

So we drove over to the Temple law offices, and then we drove around looking for a parking place, and when we finally found one, we were almost back at the County Building. Grandfather must have been doing some weighty thinking, because he didn't even complain.

Old Man Temple was out, but Grandfather cornered Junior behind his desk in that big office, and came directly to the point. "Have you gone through Pesman's papers, yet?"

"No," Junior said.

"Why not?" Grandfather wanted to know.

Junior waved his arms, and spoke as if he were reciting something. "I have no authority. I am not the executor of Pesman's estate until I receive letters of administration from the probate court. Until I am the executor I have no authority—no right—no business—to touch Pesman's property."

"I guess that's clear enough," Grandfather said. "Who do I have to see to get permission to look through his papers myself?"

Junior stared at him, and opened and closed his mouth a couple of times, and all of a sudden he was powerfully worked up about something. His face didn't turn red, like Sheriff Pilkins'—it went white. His bow tie bounced every time he swallowed, which was frequently.

"You can't," he whispered.

"Of course I can," Grandfather said. "It's in the best interest of the estate to get the murder solved, and that's what I'm trying to do. I'm not going to eat the papers. I just want to look at them."

Suddenly Junior pounded on his desk and shouted, "No!" His glasses flew across the room and bounced twice, and somehow didn't break. He kept on pounding his desk, and yelling at the top of his voice. "Everybody wants something. Boyd wants instructions. I can't give him any. The sheriff wants to put a gate up. I did, but I shouldn't have. Krohl wants to sell stock. A caretaker has to be appointed. Kruger wants to buy the animals. Mrs. Glover wants her favorite cake pan. You want to look at papers. I can't, I tell you—I can't. I have no authority—no right—no business—"

He dropped his arms onto his desk, and buried his face in them.

Grandfather stood there completely confounded, and I was feeling pretty amazed myself. We turned to tiptoe away, and met Old Man Temple at the door.

He seemed to take in the situation at a glance. "What do you want?" he said softly.

"I'd like to look at Pesman's papers."

"Tell Willie I said it's all right."

"Thanks." Grandfather said.

We left, and Old Man Temple closed the door behind us, very quietly.

"Well," I said when we got outside, "what do you think of that?"

"Up to now Junior's been leaning pretty heavily on his dad," Grandfather said. "It looks to me as if his dad is making him handle this case on his own. He's tossed Junior into it to sink or swim and I don't think he's going to swim. It's kind of a shame."

On our way back to the car Grandfather bought a box of doughnuts and a carton of milk, and he made a lunch out of that while I drove out to the Courthouse, complaining that I intentionally hit a bump whenever he tried to drink the milk. The gate was locked, but I honked the horn until I finally aroused Willie. Grandfather told him he had Temple's permission to look through the professor's papers and records, and Willie nodded, and led us up to the laboratory, and unlocked the door for us.

The laboratory took up the whole third floor of the Courthouse. Before the professor bought the place there were rooms there, but the professor had removed the partitions. All along one side were cages for the animals—forty times as many animals as the professor needed, Grandfather thought, and that side of the room looked like a zoo. The rest looked pretty much like a junk yard, except for the corner where the professor had his desk and filing cabinets, and book cases, and of course the model of the maze, which was a tremendous thing, built on legs so that it stood waist high. In the center a little circular iron staircase went up to the dome in the roof, and scattered all around the room was stuff that I suppose the professor called scientific apparatus, but which looked like junk to me. The dummies were there, too—twelve of them, made to look like men and women, and Mr. Boyd hadn't been kidding when he said they needed renovating. A stranger happening onto one of them in the maze would have been scared silly, if he didn't stay around for more than a first look, because he'd think that someone else had been lost in the maze and left there to decay. At the far end of the room were a couple of smaller mazes, built so that the partitions, or whatever they are, could be changed around. The professor liked to make an animal learn its way through one of them, and then he would change a partition or two, just to see if he could drive the animal nuts.

Grandfather sat down at the professor's desk, and I went up the circular staircase to the dome. The professor had a little table there, and a chair, and everything laid out ready for action: a pair of binoculars, some sharpened pencils, and a whole pile of mimeographed maps of the maze. When someone got into the maze the professor would write down the date and the time he started, and then he would trace his route with a pencil, probably chuckling over all the mistakes he made. Then he would record the time the person got out, or gave up, whichever the case happened to be, and he had another record ready for the file. He'd been doing that for years, which accounted for all the filing cabinets.

Of course the salesmen who wandered into the maze weren't very good specimens, because they weren't likely to go at it the way the professor wanted them to. What the professor liked to do was put a person at a certain spot in the maze—he called it "placing the specimen"—and then at a signal, which consisted of the professor sticking his head out of an open window in the dome and shouting, "Go!" the person would try to get out as fast as he could. Sometimes the person would be blindfolded until the professor got him placed, and sometimes he wouldn't be. The professor usually offered a cash bonus if the person could find his way out within a certain time, but I never heard of anyone winning one. I know I didn't.

It was the first time I'd ever been up there in the dome, and naturally I was curious about how I'd looked when I was running in the maze. I took the binoculars and had myself a good bird's-eye view of the thing. It was possible to see into most of the alleys running towards the highway, but not those going the other way, because the hedges were too high. The professor wouldn't have had much trouble following a specimen's route, though, because of the intersections. It made me mad to think of all the times the professor had sat up there watching me try to find my way out.

I took a map and a pencil, and went to work to see if I could trace the one route that led from the Courthouse out to the highway. I worked at it for maybe twenty minutes, but there were so many alleys, and the turns were so complicated, that I was always losing my place when I looked from the maze to the map and back again. I gave up, and went back down to the laboratory and put my favorite guinea pig into a maze to see how he would make out. He scurried around a little, then he came back to where I was and tried to climb out, so I put him back in his cage.

Grandfather was taking the file drawers one at a time, and putting them on the professor's desk, and pawing through them. I went over to ask him how he was making out, and then I saw the look on his face and decided not to. I went downstairs to look for Willie, and maybe have a game of checkers, but he was outside on a chaise lounge looking at a book, and I decided not to bother him.

I went back to the laboratory and put a white rat into the model of the big maze, and that rat went through the thing so fast that all I could do was stand there and blink. I rewarded it with a handful of oats, and then I went over to tell Grandfather about it.

"You can throw all this stuff out," I said. "None of it is any good. The experiments were rigged."

"How is that?" he wanted to know.

"Come here and I'll show you," I said.

I tried another rat, and it breezed through the maze as easily as the first one had done. Grandfather shrugged his shoulders, and went back to the filing cabinet.

"Don't you see the catch?" I asked.

"It's a pretty smart rat," he said.

"Sure. It's also a trained rat. The professor did a lot of experiments comparing rats with people, but he used different people. The rats were always the same. It wasn't a fair test."

"I still say it's a smart rat," Grandfather said. "If I remember correctly, you had quite a few shots at the maze. How does it happen that you didn't get trained?"

He had me there, so I went back up to the dome and had another try at finding a path through the maze. Just as I was beginning to make progress I heard Grandfather whistle, so I dropped everything and went tearing back down the stairs to see what had happened.

Grandfather had a folder on the desk, and in the folder was a pile of account statements from Strobel, Ross, Beal and Larkins. Grandfather was comparing a couple of them, and he let out another whistle as I walked up.

"Maybe I'll have to take a closer look at this stock market business," he said.

"Why's that?" I asked.

"Look here. March twenty-second the professor bought a thousand shares of Alachron Corporation. He paid twenty-five and a half, which I take to mean twenty-five and a half dollars per share. April third he sold a thousand shares of Alachron Corporation at thirty-nine and three eighths. If I understand this correctly, in less than two weeks he made almost fourteen thousand dollars. I always thought the professor was a dunce about practical things, and here he made more money in two weeks than I ever have in two years."

"Uh huh," I said. "I also see that if he bought a thousand shares at— what was it?"

"Twenty-five and a half."

"Then it cost him twenty-five and a half thousand dollars. All this proves is that you can make fourteen thousand dollars in two weeks if you have twenty-five thousand dollars to make it with."

"Still, two hundred and fifty dollars would have brought a profit of a hundred and forty."

He picked up the next page, which was the last one in the pile. "This must be the stock Krohl was talking about," he said. "Roth Mining. The professor bought two thousand shares at nineteen and an eighth. He put all the money he took out of Alachron Corporation into Roth Mining. Johnny, call up Krohl and ask him what Roth Mining is selling for now."

"Glad to," I said, "if the telephone hasn't been disconnected."

"Junior doesn't have the authority," Grandfather said.

The telephone was working, so I called Strobel, Ross, Beal and Lar-kins. No one answered at the office, but I got Jerry Krohl at home and told him Grandfather wanted to know what Roth Mining was selling at.

"For God's sake!" he said. "Why that stock?"

"Oh, he doesn't want to buy it," I said. "He's been going over Profes-sor Pesman's papers, and he was just curious about how much money the professor has lost on it."

"He shouldn't have lost any money on it," Krohl said. "He bought it at—I don't remember, now."

"Nineteen and something," I said.

"Yes. A month after he bought it, it was at twenty-three, and he could have had a fast profit of over seven thousand, but he wouldn't sell. I don't remember where Roth closed today, but yesterday it closed at seven and three fourths."

"Thanks," I said. "That's what we wanted to know."

I went upstairs and told Grandfather, and he whistled again and got out his pencil. "On second thought, maybe I better stay out of the stock mar-ket. First the professor made fourteen thousand, and now he's lost nearly twenty-four thousand. No wonder Krohl was hot about selling it."

"He said the professor could have made over seven thousand in a month," I said. "Only he wouldn't sell it."

"Pesman was a bit pig-headed at times—most of the time," Grandfa-ther said. "It was the same way with his scientific experiments. The thing had to come out just the way he wanted it to, and if it didn't he'd change things around until it did. He probably thought he could manipulate the stock market the same way he did things in his laboratory."

"Just like matching trained rats against untrained people," I said.

"Krohl seems to have given him good advice about stocks. In the last five years I couldn't find any other place where he lost money. I guess when a man starts playing with the stock market, he'd better know a lot about it, or stick with the ideas of someone who does."

"What about the Modern Merchandising Corporation?" I asked.

"Nothing," Grandfather said. He put the folder back in a file drawer, and said, "That's funny. Go ask Willie if the professor kept some of his records someplace else."

Having a conversation with Willie was always a strain, but when I finished and got his nodding and head shaking tabulated, I was pretty sure that if there were records anywhere but in the laboratory Willie didn't know about them.

Grandfather had to think that over, and then he said, "Call Temple—no, I'd better call him myself."

H went to the kitchen to telephone, and I went after Willie to get the laboratory locked up again. Grandfather's call didn't take long, because when I got back he had also called Mom to tell her we'd be late for supper. "I want to stop and talk with Jones," he said.

"What's missing?" I asked him.

"I can't find a scrap of information about the professor's dealings with Jones. The professor saved everything else, so you'd think there would be something there. All Temple knows about it is that the professor would tell him each year what the income from the farm land amounted to, and he'd use that in figuring the professor's income tax. If he needed any more information, he'd ask Jones. So that's what I'm going to do—ask Jones."

We found Jones in his barn, milking his cows—or rather, watching his milking machines milk his cows. Grandfather was a long time talking with him, because Jones was as slow about conversation as he was about everything else, and he was always breaking off to empty one of the milking machines. There were four cats that followed him around everywhere, waiting for him to spill a little milk for them, which he usually did. He offered me a glass of warm milk, but this is one product that I cannot enjoy so close to the source of supply.

Grandfather explained what he wanted, and then Jones went to empty a milking machine, and when he came back Grandfather explained again, and then Jones had to empty another milking machine, and I began to think that the conversation would last as long as the cows did.

"What records?" Jones said finally.

He was a tall, muscular man who moved slowly, and thought slowly, and he had never been known to laugh at anything. There were those who thought that this was why he was such a good farmer—he was never in a hurry, so he did everything the way it ought to be done.

"You've been farming the professor's land for him on shares," Grandfather said, "but he doesn't have any records of it."

"I guess he doesn't," Jones said.

"Then how did he keep track of the business?"

"I keep the records," Jones said. "Always have. He never knew anything about farming."

"That seems like an odd arrangement," Grandfather said. "If it were me, I'd want something in writing so I could know what was going on. Are those records in order now?"

"I guess they're as much in order as they've ever been," Jones said.

"Because someone will have to check them over—audit them, maybe."

Jones scowled. "Why all the fuss about records? There never was any trouble before."

"The professor was never dead before," Grandfather said.

We left Lyle Jones to his cows, and drove home for our late supper. It was a welcome meal for both of us—for Grandfather because he hadn't had any solid food since breakfast and for me because I always welcome any meal.

After supper Grandfather asked me how I would like another trip to Ohio. "I'd like it fine," I said.

"I wouldn't," Grandfather said, and telephoned Sheriff Pilkins.

"What's the word on the Modern Merchandising Corporation?" he asked.

He listened, grunting a couple of times, from which I gathered that there wasn't any word.

"That so," he said finally. "I went through the professor's personal papers this afternoon, so you won't have to do that. Why, don't you think I can read? Suit yourself. The reason I called you, I was just wondering which of your deputies you're going to send down to Southern Ohio University."

The telephone squawked a couple of times, and went silent. "Did he faint?" I whispered. Grandfather chuckled. "Johnny wants to know if you fainted."

Evidently the sheriff didn't appreciate that, and no doubt he was still mad because we'd jolted him out of his chipper mood that afternoon. What followed was an argument that put at least ten years' depreciation on the wire between Wiston and Borgville. At times I could hear what the sheriff was saying clear across the living room, and before they finished I was wondering how long it would be before the neighbors complained about Grandfather.

"All right," Grandfather said finally. "Since you won't send anyone, I guess I'll have to go myself. I'll be leaving tonight."

That brought a good measure of silence. Then the sheriff told Grandfather he could go anywhere he wanted to, and he didn't care where, and he mentioned a place or two by way of illustration.

Grandfather waited until the sheriff had gotten himself completely unwound. "As long as you feel that way," he said, "I suppose anything I turn up on this trip should be given to the State Police." The sheriff, who was roaring again, said Grandfather could give his information to the State Police, or the F.B.I., or the Girl Scouts for all he cared.

"There's just one problem," Grandfather said. "All these trips to Ohio are costing me money. It was nice of you to reimburse Johnny for his expenses, but you haven't offered to do that for me. You're trying to sit tight because you think you have the murderer, but you wouldn't have him if I hadn't paid for a trip to Ohio. I have a hunch that this next trip will turn up something just as important. If it does, I intend to ask the county Board of Supervisors to reimburse me for both trips. Of course some of the members may want to ask a few questions about why the official law enforcement officer of this county is so inefficient that an outsider has to step in and do his work. I'm tipping you off ahead of time, so you can start getting some answers ready."

That brought another explosion. They kept at it for maybe twenty minutes longer, until the sheriff suddenly decided it might be a real good idea to send a deputy down to Southern Ohio University.

"Tonight," Grandfather said.

"Send anyone but Steve Carling," Grandfather said, which started another argument, though I think the sheriff had already decided to send Roy Foster.

Finally they got things arranged to the point where neither of them could think of anything more to argue about, and Grandfather hung up, and got out his handkerchief and mopped his forehead.

"This case can't be settled until that business about the Modern Merchandising Corporation is cleared up," he said. "And anyone but an idiot should be able to see that. Pilkins—"

"I know," I said. "Sheriff Pilkins is an idiot."

CHAPTER X

Thursday morning Grandfather stayed in his room and rocked. Since his room is right over the kitchen I listened to him while I ate, and the rocking chair was hitting a steady creaking pace that was so far below par for him that I wondered if he was sick. I went up and took a look, but he didn't look sick, and when I asked him how he felt there wasn't anything feeble about the way he threw a slipper at me.

About ten o'clock, when I came in for a snack, he'd picked up considerable speed, and when I looked in at eleven-thirty to see what Mom was fixing for lunch his chair was making an awful racket, and Mom was worrying about the carpet.

He braked to a stop when I told him lunch was ready, and then on the way to the kitchen he stopped to look at the mail and found a bill from one of the plumbers, and he said he wasn't hungry and went back upstairs to rock some more. He came down later, though, and finished up what was left of Mom's beef roast, and then he asked me to drive him to Wiston.

"You'd better stay away from that house," I said. "Every time you go there something happens."

"You reason like Pilkins," he said. "My staying away won't keep things from happening. Anyway, that's not where I'm going."

Mr. Snubbs came just as we were leaving, bringing Grandfather the morning paper. Grandfather hadn't been in to borrow it that week, and Mr. Snubbs thought he must have broken his leg, or had a stroke, or something. Grandfather thanked him, and said he was too busy to be thinking about newspapers, but he might find time to read it that evening.

We started for Wiston, and when we reached the maze Grandfather asked me to pull over for a moment.

"You can't get in from this side," I told him. "There's a gate. I saw it yesterday when I was up in the dome."

"That gate is what I want to see," Grandfather said.

So I stopped, and we went to look at the gate. It was a stout metal one, and it was fastened with a great big shiny padlock, but the gate was only about three feet high.

"That's the way Junior does things," Grandfather said. "He's too shy to come right out and tell anyone to keep out. He'd rather beat around the bush, and hint a little. This gate is a hint."

"That's probably all that's needed, now that the signs are gone," I said. "Most people know too much about this place to try to do any sightseeing here."

Grandfather stepped over the gate, and I followed him. "The sheriff has left his tape," he said. "Anyone interested could walk right in to where the murder happened, and tromp all over the place. And if the murderer's left something there, he can hop over that gate and pick it up any time he feels like it."

"If he'd left something, the sheriff would have found it," I said.

"If it was a foot high, and one of his men happened to fall over it, he would have found it. It seems to me that there's got to be something to learn here, but darned if I can think what it is."

He kicked at the gravel path a couple of times, and scratched his head, and then he said, "Let's go."

We went first to the Temple law offices, where Grandfather wanted to find out if Junior had the new addresses of Mr. Boyd, and Mrs. Glover, and Pete Kruger. Junior blushed when we walked in, and apologized for his conduct of the day before. "My nerves must have been bothering me," he said.

"That's all right," Grandfather said. "My nerves bother me sometimes."

"They do?" Junior said, sounding pleased.

"Where's your father this afternoon?" Grandfather asked.

"He's out of town looking for a witness," Junior said.

"Is he just about ready for Vaughan's hearing?"

"I don't know," Junior said. "He doesn't tell me much about it."

Junior did have the addresses, because he was going to have to send out salary checks, and severance pay, and the thousand-dollar bequests when he eventually got the authority. He gave Grandfather the list, which also included Willie's name and this was a matter of some interest because there was a last name. Willie Brandt.

I looked at Grandfather, and Grandfather looked at me, and when we got outside I said. "I've heard that name before."

"You and everyone else," Grandfather said.

"Who is he?"

"Willy Brandt is the mayor of West Berlin. Only it isn't spelled Willie."

"Do you suppose Willie is related to him?"

"No," Grandfather said. "I don't suppose so."

We went first to see Mrs. Glover. She'd found herself a little basement apartment, and she said she liked it fine, especially the kitchen. Her attitude hadn't changed a bit, because the first thing she wanted to know was whether we'd had lunch. We told her we had, but she brought in pieces of apple pie anyway, and coffee for Grandfather and milk for me.

"How are things going?" Grandfather asked.

"Just fine," Mrs. Glover said.

"Found yourself another job yet?"

"I haven't even looked," she said.

It could have been my imagination, but I thought she blushed. I'd never thought of a woman her age as having any need to blush, but then she didn't seem to look as old as I'd thought she was. She'd done something to her hair, which had always been a little on the stringy side. Now it was curled, with a nice wave over her forehead, and when she came to get my plate I noticed she was wearing nail polish.

She took the dishes to the kitchen, and then she sat down and asked Grandfather what was on his mind. "I know you didn't just come to pay a social call on an old woman like me," she said.

"When a woman cooks the way you do, her age isn't important," Grandfather said.

She smiled, and told him flattery would get him nowhere.

"What I was wondering," Grandfather said, "was if there might be something that happened the day the professor was murdered that you didn't remember when the sheriff talked with you."

She shook her head. "That stupid deputy—what's his name, Steve something or other? Anyway, he kept after me for an hour, but I couldn't think of anything. It was just a day like any other day."

"Supposing we try again," Grandfather said. "What happened right after lunch?"

"Well, Mr. Krohl came while we were eating lunch, and as soon as the professor finished he took him up to the laboratory to talk. I did the dishes, and then I mixed up a cake and put it in the oven, and then—"

"Just a moment. You did see Mr. Krohl leave, didn't you?"

"Oh. I saw him through the kitchen window. I suppose I was still doing dishes, because the window is right over the sink."

"Good. He drove away—"

"Pete had to let him out, because the gate was locked."

"And then what happened?"

"I put the cake in the oven, and then I mopped the kitchen floor, and then I went down to the freezer to get some pork chops for supper, and—I don't remember what all I did. I kept busy, I know that much."

"When did you first hear that the professor was doing a special experiment?"

"Evan told me when the professor didn't come down for supper."

"You didn't think that was unusual?"

"It didn't happen very often, but it wasn't exactly unusual."

"During the early afternoon did you look out at the maze at any time?"

She shook her head. "I don't believe I left the kitchen once, except when I went down to the freezer. I never paid any attention to the maze anyway. It was always there, and it always looked the same, and if I had happened into the living room and looked out, well, I wouldn't have been able to see anything from the ground floor. The hedges are too high."

"Then you spent the whole afternoon in the kitchen."

"No, but I was there until after my cake was finished. I went upstairs— oh, maybe about three o'clock—and took a nap until it was time to start supper."

"And you didn't see the professor again after lunch?"

"No," she said. "I already told the sheriff—"

"I know," Grandfather said. "I wanted to hear it again. I think I understand how it was, now, but there's one thing that isn't clear to me. What about the bell?"

"Well, what about it?"

"Did you hear it ring while you were in the kitchen?"

"I don't remember. I just never paid any attention to it. It was no concern of mine."

"I know that," Grandfather said. "But this may be very important, so I want you to try to remember. The professor left the dining room and went upstairs with Mr. Krohl. Then Mr. Krohl came down again and left, and by that time you were in the kitchen, doing the dishes. Now think—you made your cake, and put it in the oven, and did some work around the kitchen. You could hear the bell from the kitchen, couldn't you?"

"I could hear it, but I never paid any attention to it, except that night when it kept on ringing."

"I understand that. But I want you to try and remember whether you heard it that afternoon. Let's try it a step at a time. Did you hear the bell ring while you were mixing up your cake?"

She thought for a moment. "No. I'm sure I didn't. Of course if it rang while I was using the mixer I might not have noticed it."

"But you didn't use the mixer very long, did you?" Grandfather said. "All right now—you put the cake in the oven, and did some other work while you were waiting for it to bake. Did you hear the bell?"

"I couldn't have heard it while I was in the basement."

"But you weren't down there very long," Grandfather said. "Just think about being in the kitchen. Did the bell ring?"

She shook her head. Then she sat up straight, and said, "Oh!"

"Tell me about it," Grandfather said.

"I was in the pantry, rearranging the shelves, and I thought I heard the timer go off. So I went to see, and the timer still had twenty minutes to go. I thought I was hearing things, but what I heard must have been the bell."

"What time was that?" Grandfather asked.

"I don't know exactly."

"Well, your cake had already been in the oven—how long?"

She thought about it for a moment. "I suppose it happened a little before two o'clock."

"Did you hear the bell ring again?"

"No."

"At least we've accomplished something," Grandfather said. "Now let's try again."

She didn't want to try again, and she might have said so if the doorbell hadn't rung just then. She went to the door, and it was Mr. Boyd. He grabbed her and was about to kiss her when he noticed that she had company.

"Oh, it's you," he said. "Has my blushing bride told you the news?"

"Evan!" she said.

"Well, it isn't the sort of thing we can keep a secret. The license will be in the paper anyway, so we might as well spread the word around and rig in all the wedding presents we can get." He turned to Grandfather. "We're getting married next week."

"Congratulations," Grandfather said.

"Thanks. I decided I couldn't get along without Ruth's cooking. I can't afford to hire her to cook for me, so marrying her is the next best thing. Did you notice what she's done to her hair? Makes her look thirty years younger. I was afraid the gal at the county clerk's office would think she was under age, and make her get her mother's consent."

"You're looking pretty good yourself," Grandfather said.

It was a fact. He was wearing new overalls, which was an article of clothing I'd never seen him have on. They made him look a few years younger, and for once he didn't smell like Bailey's Bar.

"I've got a job," he said. "The Wiston Manufacturing Company is taking a chance on me as a night watchman. It's a funny feeling, earning an honest living for a change, and I'll have to admit that I get other feelings out of it, too—especially in the legs, about four A.M. I suppose it isn't much of a job, but it's a start. We both have money saved, and if things go well we'll buy ourselves a vine-covered cottage and settle down and raise a large family."

Now Mrs. Glover really was blushing. "Evan! We're old enough to be grandparents right now."

"All right—we'll raise ourselves a large family of grandchildren. I don't believe I asked you what you were molesting my bride about."

"Just asking a few questions," Grandfather said.

"That's what I figured. I thought the sheriff had the murder solved."

"He thinks so, too," Grandfather said. "But I've known Pilkins to be wrong so many times that when he makes up his mind about something I just naturally think the opposite. I have a few questions for you, too."

"Fire away. I don't have to be at work until nine."

"What I'm really interested in," Grandfather said, "are these bells that ring when someone goes into the maze. There's one downstairs in the hallway, and there's one up in the laboratory, and it seems to me that I've heard of a third one."

"It's in the prof's bedroom."

"Let's see, now—after the professor told you he was going to do a special experiment, and didn't want to be bothered, you went to your room."

"Right," Mr. Boyd said. "Let me say further that I told a lie when the sheriff asked me about that. I told him I was reading. I wasn't. I was very slowly and painlessly getting drunk. I never really got drunk, but I always had a lot of satisfaction out of trying. I don't suppose that's news to you, and I never cared what anyone thought anyway. But now I do, so I'm going on the wagon permanently."

"I wish you luck," Grandfather said. "Could you hear any of those bells from your room?"

"I could hear the one in the prof's bedroom faintly if I happened to be listening carefully. That day I wasn't in any condition to be listening."

"Then you didn't hear it ring."

"I didn't hear anything."

"Try thinking about it," Grandfather suggested. "It could be important."

"Thinking wouldn't help. If I heard any bells that afternoon, they weren't the prof's alarm bells."

"Supposing you had heard one. What would you have done?"

"Nothing. The prof was in the laboratory, or at least I thought he was, and I'd have thought that he would take care of it. And that's all I can tell you."

"I can't expect any more than that," Grandfather said. "Thanks. Thank you, Ruth. Are you two having a regular wedding?"

"A very quiet affair, with the minimum number of witnesses," Boyd said. "Would you like to be one of them?"

"Glad to be," Grandfather said. "When is it?"

"That isn't settled yet. We still have to find a minister disreputable enough to accept the job. I'll let you know. And I appreciate it."

Mrs. Glover started getting food out for Mr. Boyd and we had to slip away in a hurry to keep her from feeding us a second time. We went back to my jalopy, but I didn't start the motor. "Why all the fuss about bells?" I asked Grandfather.

"The murderer had to get into the maze, and out again," Grandfather said. "There are only two places he could do it—one by the highway and one by the house. If he got by the house, he had to come through the car gate, which was locked, and through the yard, where Pete and Nat were working."

"He couldn't have done that without being seen," I said.

"Then he came in from the highway, and he rang the bell twice, once when he went in, and once when he came out. The bell Mrs. Glover heard was Vaughan entering the maze. She'd gone upstairs before he came out. If Pilkins gets to thinking about bells Vaughan will be in more trouble than he already is, because Mrs. Glover's testimony will just about prove that nobody but Vaughan rang a bell that afternoon. The way I see it, that bell had to ring twice between—oh, say a quarter to one and a quarter to two. Why didn't Mrs. Glover hear it?"

"She wasn't listening."

"I think she would have heard it if it rang. She heard it later, when she was in the pantry. That just doesn't make sense, and I don't like things that don't make sense."

"Maybe the murderer climbed over the hedge," I said. "He could have tossed one of those rope ladders over it, easy, and then—"

"And then he would have been way out at the side of the maze, and his chances of finding the professor from there would be about one in a million. Let's go see Pete."

Pete had taken a furnished room way over on the other side of town. I had to ask for directions at a filling station, and then as we passed the County Building Sheriff Pilkins came driving out of the parking lot. He waved, and pulled out and followed us.

"Take it easy, Johnny," Grandfather said. "He'd probably love to give us a ticket."

"You could put it on your expense account," I said. "Anyway, he couldn't do it in town, could he? Does he have the authority, or the right, or the business—"

"He's no Junior Temple," Grandfather said. "The town is in his county, and he's liable to try, whether he has the right or not."

He stayed right behind us until we found Pete's house, and when we parked he did, too, and got out to ask us what we were up to.

"I'm calling on an old friend," Grandfather said.

"I think I'll call on him, too. He's a friend of mine, isn't he?"

"Does this nonsense come under the heading of a criminal investigation?"

"It might," the sheriff said. "Depends on who your friend is."

"No wonder crime runs rampant in this county," Grandfather said.

The sheriff's face did a nice color change, be he didn't say anything, and when we went up the steps to the house he followed along.

Pete's landlady, who was not skinny, came to the door and told us, all smiles, that she thought Mr. Kruger was in, and his room was the first on the right at the top of the stairs. Then she waddled away, probably hoping that Mr. Kruger would not be entertaining riff-raff like us every day.

"Kruger, eh?" the sheriff said. "I've been wanting to talk with my old friend Pete."

He pushed ahead of us going up the stairs, and when we got to the top he was already knocking at Pete's door. Pete opened the door, and the sheriff said, "Hello, Pete," and what happened after that had to be seen to be believed.

One look at the sheriff, and Pete's face turned the color of those sheets that are washed by Brand X on television. His mouth dropped open. He half raised his hands, and then he backed clear across the room and dropped onto the bed, sobbing like a kid who's just had a going over with a razor strap.

The sheriff stood in the doorway with his own mouth open wider than I would have recommended, considering the condition of his teeth. Grandfather shoved him out of the way and went over to have a look at Pete, and I gave him another push to get the door closed.

"I'll be darned," the sheriff said. "What's chewing him?"

"What's the matter, Pete?" Grandfather asked.

Pete's wrinkled old face was screwed up like a howling baby's. He stopped sobbing long enough to say, "I knew I shouldn't have done it." Then he started in again, with more volume.

"Done what?" Grandfather asked. And the sheriff echoed, "Done what?"

Pete fought for his breath, and managed to get out, "I knew he'd catch me," and went on crying. I felt like stepping outside until it was over with. If Professor Pesman had been around, he'd have said that a crying old man was an unwholesome influence on a young person.

"Cut it out, Pete," the sheriff said. "If you're innocent, you've got nothing to worry about."

"I'm not innocent!" Pete howled.

Grandfather told the sheriff to sit down and shut up, and he sent me down the hall to the bathroom after a glass of cold water. He tried to get Pete to drink this, but the sobs coming up were all Pete's swallowing apparatus could cope with, and finally Grandfather got disgusted and threw the rest of the water into Pete's face. Pete came off the bed bubbling like a drowning man, but at least it stopped his crying. Grandfather tossed him a towel, and he mopped his face off, and gulped out one last sob, and said,

"All right. I'll come quietly."

"Where are we going?" Grandfather asked.

Pete stared at him. "Didn't you come to arrest me?"

"Any particular reason you should be arrested?" Grandfather asked.

Pete pointed at the sheriff. "*He* knows, or he wouldn't be here." And with that he sat down and wouldn't say another word.

Grandfather and I were too amazed to do anything but stand there and stare at him, and the sheriff, who was sitting on the one chair in the room, opened and closed his mouth a few times while he scratched with one finger at the little bald spot he has on top of his head.

"Sheriff Pilkins," Grandfather said finally, making it sound so official that it dripped, "do you suppose you could parole this man in my custody for a while?"

"What's that?" the sheriff asked. Grandfather scowled at him. "Oh," the sheriff said. "Well, I guess I could manage that. I have a man at both the front and back doors, so he couldn't get away. I'll be downstairs if you need me."

He went out, not happily, and closed the door.

Grandfather waited a minute, and then he said, "See if he's gone, Johnny."

I opened the door a crack, and the sheriff, who had his ear to the keyhole, nearly tumbled into the room.

"Yep, he's gone," I said, pushing the door shut.

"Good," Grandfather said. "Now, then, Pete, if we put our heads together we just might be able to beat this thing. Got any ideas?

Pete shook his head, and looked as if he was about to start bawling again. "It's no use. He's caught me with the goods."

"That does make it tough," Grandfather said. "I'm sure there's a way out, if we can just think of it."

We thought. At least, Pete went through the motions of thinking. Grandfather and I stood and watched him.

Suddenly he snapped his fingers. "I got it! I'll give Herman to you. When the sheriff searches me I'll be clean, and he's too dumb to ever think of searching you."

Grandfather turned to me with as close a thing to a blank look as I've ever seen him offer.

"Sounds like a good idea to me," I said. "You've often told me the sheriff is an idiot. We might as well take advantage of it."

"I suppose so," Grandfather said. "All right, I'll take Herman."

"This is real nice of you, Mr. Rastin," Pete said. He reached into his pocket, and handed Grandfather the white mouse. "I knew I shouldn't have taken him," he said, "but I just couldn't leave him there in that cage. Willie doesn't really know how to look after animals, and anyway, Herman needs more than just a little food and water every day. He's too used to having, well, companionship. He'd know Willie didn't have any personal interest in him."

"You're absolutely right," Grandfather said, though from the expression on his face you'd have thought Pete had just handed him a rattlesnake. "Will he stay in my pocket?"

"Oh, he likes it in pockets. It's always nice and warm in pockets."

"Right," Grandfather said. "Into the pocket it is. Johnny, go call the sheriff."

Sheriff Pilkins backed away from the door as I opened it. For a moment I couldn't tell if he was mad enough to blow his top, or just trying not to laugh, and I finally decided it was both. We waited long enough for me to have gone downstairs and back, and then I opened the door again.

"Sheriff," Grandfather said, "You've got the wrong man."

"Nonsense," the sheriff said. "I never get the wrong man."

"You've got the wrong man this time. Search him, and see for yourself."

The sheriff grabbed Pete, and turned all of his pockets inside out. "He's got it hid somewhere in the room," he said. "Johnny, give me a hand with the bed."

We tore the bed apart, and then we took drawers out and emptied them onto the floor, and then we tossed the clothing out of the closet and went through those pockets, and then the sheriff, who was really enjoying himself, started over again and made Pete take off his pants just to be sure he didn't have the mouse cached somewhere in a pants leg. Pete's old face had a real glow of satisfaction, and every time the sheriff went to look somewhere else he snickered at him.

"Well, Pete," the sheriff said finally, "I guess I owe you an apology. I don't see how I could have made such a mistake. I'll have to fire the deputy I had tailing you."

"Oh, don't do that," Pete said. "Everybody makes mistakes."

"That's true," the sheriff said. "But my men never make more than one. And you, Rastin, I don't think you're entirely clean in this matter, and I'm going to keep my eye on you." He went out slamming the door.

Grandfather handed Herman back to Pete. Then he turned his pocket inside out, and brushed it off. Herman ran up Pete's arm, and ducked inside his shirt collar.

"You're a real friend, Mr. Rastin," Pete said. "It sure was lucky for me you happened along just now."

"That's all right, Pete," Grandfather said. "I saw the sheriff stop here and I wondered what he was up to."

"Anytime I can do something for you—"

"I'll let you know," Grandfather promised.

Sheriff Pilkins was waiting for us out front. "I should have searched you," he said to Grandfather. "I could have pulled you in for possessing stolen property. It was the chance of a lifetime, and I may never get another one like it."

We got into my jalopy, and Grandfather rolled down the window and leaned out. "The last laugh is on you," he said. "While you were tearing the room apart, Pete slipped the mouse into your pocket."

I drove away, and just before I rounded the corner both of us looked back. The sheriff was still standing there on the sidewalk, but now he had all of his pockets turned inside out.

CHAPTER XI

A few blocks down the street Grandfather asked me to pull over and park. "I want to do some thinking," he said.

"That isn't very complimentary to my driving," I said.

"It isn't your driving that bothers me. It's this confounded city traffic."

We were driving down a quiet residential street. We'd met only one moving vehicle in the last three blocks, and all the city traffic in sight consisted of a few parked cars. Either Professor Pesman's murder was getting on Grandfather's nerves, or he hadn't any idea what to do next and was stalling for time. Knowing Grandfather's nerves as I did, I thought he was stalling.

I parked, and a minute later the sheriff drove by, pretending not to see us. Grandfather mussed up his eyebrows, and wrinkled his forehead, and scratched at his head a couple of times, and finally told me I might as well drive on. "I can't do any real thinking without a rocking chair," he said.

"Shall we go back to Pete's place?"

"Why?"

"You didn't ask him if he heard the bell."

"He couldn't have heard the bell. He was outside all afternoon."

"He could have seen something," I said.

"He said he didn't, but I'll talk to him again later. Preferably when he isn't harboring a menagerie."

I said that it was an exaggeration to call the possession of one white mouse harboring a menagerie, and Grandfather said that depended on how much of a menagerie the mouse was harboring. He wiped his hand off on his pant leg, and then he brushed off his pant leg and said we might as well get started.

"Where to?" I asked.

"To the college. I want to find out a few things about this Professor Collins."

"It's after four o'clock. Will the college be open?"

"The surest way to find out if something is open is to go there and try to get in."

For a few minutes it looked as if the college was open to everyone but us. Dean Morris's office was empty except for his secretary—who wasn't nearly as pretty as the secretary of the president of Landsdorf College had been, but I suppose deans aren't able to compete with presidents in such matters. The idea that two such disreputable-looking characters as us should expect to see the dean without an appointment seemed to shock her. She thought she might be able to work us into his schedule in a couple of weeks, but she wouldn't come right out and promise.

Grandfather leaned over her desk, and said in a half whisper, "This is police business. I'll have to see the dean immediately."

She got up quickly and backed away from her desk, as though she wasn't quite sure which side of the police business we might be on, and when she'd put a safe distance between us she turned and scooted into a private office.

We never saw her again.

A man stuck his head around the door and looked us over cautiously. When he'd convinced himself that we weren't waiting with drawn revolvers, he came out and said he was Dean Morris, and he was extremely busy, but of course he was happy to cooperate with the police in any reasonable way, and wouldn't we come in.

He arranged chairs for us, and then he went behind his desk and stood there, looking us over again and getting more puzzled all the time. "Police business?" he said finally.

"Unofficial," Grandfather said, which I thought was unnecessary. He was wearing a red shirt, open at the collar, and the green plaid suspenders I gave him for Christmas, and I was wearing slacks and a T shirt, neither of them very clean, and anyone but a blind man would have known at one glance that whatever it was we were up to couldn't be official.

"Also," Grandfather said, "absolutely confidential."

"Oh, absolutely," the dean said.

I looked around for the secretary, but either she'd slipped out the back way, or she was hiding in the closet. The dean seated himself, and offered Grandfather a cigarette from one of those fancy carved boxes.

"No, thank you," Grandfather said.

The dean smiled at me, and said, "And you, young man—I suppose you're too young to smoke."

Nothing irks me quite as much as being called, "young man," because the person that does it is usually hinting that I might not be out of diapers yet. So I got up and helped myself to a cigarette, and I said, "No sir, I don't smoke, but I'm saving them up for when I'm old enough."

That startled the dean so much that he lit his lighter before he realized that he hadn't taken a cigarette for himself. He took one, and got it lit, and then he said, "Police business. I hope none of our students have gotten into trouble."

"Not that I know of," Grandfather said.

"Not one of the faculty, surely."

"That I wouldn't know about."

That was the logical moment for him to throw us out, and he was big enough to do it, but he didn't. I suppose he was curious.

"Do you know a Professor James Collins?" Grandfather asked.

"Don't tell me Professor Collins is in trouble with the police!"

"Probably not," Grandfather said. "The police have to be very careful before they take any action where such a distinguished man is concerned, and I'm making a preliminary investigation. I understand that Professor Collins is in town at the invitation of the college."

"He is," the dean said. "Or rather, he's here at my personal invitation."

"And you've offered him a job."

"I've offered him the *position*," the dean said, "of head of our physics department."

"Mind telling me how you happened to offer him that position?" Grandfather asked.

"Would you mind telling me what possible connection that could have with police business?"

"I'll tell you just this much," Grandfather said. "Professor Collins turned up here in Wiston at a very peculiar time, and I intend to find out why. Is there any special secret about your offering him this job?"

"Certainly not. Our Professor William Alford, who is Chairman of our Psychology Department, met Professor Collins at the Midwest Conference on Science Education, which was held in Chicago last month. Professor Collins mentioned that he intended to leave Southern Ohio University, and that he was considering offers from several schools. Bill—Professor Alford—told him that the chairmanship of our physics department would be open, because Professor Abbott retires at the end of the summer, and he thought Professor Collins seemed interested. He suggested that I contact him, and I was happy to do so, because Professor Collins is an excellent man with an international reputation. I'll admit that I did not expect him to consider my offer seriously, because Wiston is obviously unable to match the salary and facilities of larger schools, but many men do feel that a smaller community and a smaller school provide a more congenial atmosphere in which to work. At any rate, he is interested. He spent a week with us, and now he's back again to consider our offer further. He promised me a decision by early next week, and frankly I very much hope that he will accept. Does that cover the situation?"

"Tolerably well," Grandfather said. "My understanding is that you had lunch with him a week ago last Tuesday."

The dean opened his desk calendar. "That's correct. We lunched at the faculty club."

"And you were with him—until when?"

The dean consulted the calendar again. "I see that I had a two o'clock appointment, and my recollection is that I returned here shortly before two. Since I'd walked over, I'd say that we parted at the club a little after one-thirty."

"Thank you," Grandfather said. "I guess that's all. Except for one thing. In case Professor Collins doesn't take the job, do you have someone else lined up for it?"

"I have several other men in mind."

"That's just as well," Grandfather said, "because you're going to need them."

"You mean Professor Collins—the police business—"

"I mean he won't take the job, and never intended to when he came here. Come on, Johnny."

The dean let us out of his office by the back way. His excuse was that our call was supposed to be confidential, but I think he was worried about the impression we'd make on anyone else waiting to see him. We walked down a long hallway and went down a flight of stairs, and got out of the building by a side door without any trouble. That is except for when a man mistook Grandfather for a janitor and stopped him to ask why his waste basket was never emptied.

From there I drove Grandfather over to Professor Alford's house, and Mrs. Alford said she wasn't expecting him home before evening. She thought we might find him at his office, but Grandfather telephoned, and his office didn't know where he was, either. I told Grandfather that it was a good time as any to be starting for home, because my built-in chronometer was informing me that supper time should be happening any minute, and Grandfather said he also telephoned Mom and told her we wouldn't be home for supper.

"This skipping meals may be all right for you," I said, "but I haven't been eating for as many years as you have."

Grandfather said that if my present habits were any indication, I'd have to live a lot longer than he had before I stopped being hungry. "But if you're going to make an issue of it," he said, "we'll go up town and find a place to eat."

I parked just out of the business district, where there wasn't any parking limit. Grandfather grumbled, and said we might as well have left the car in Borgville, but I didn't care. Those two parking tickets had unnerved me. I didn't resent the fact that Wiston was a growing town, but I didn't want it to grow at my expense.

As so happens when you start out to do something with Grandfather, he got sidetracked. First he had to stop at a real estate office to ask a young man to take a look at his Wiston house and tell him what he might be able to sell it for. And then he had to go over to the branch office of Strobel, Ross, Beal and Larkins to buy some stock. I wouldn't have believed it if I hadn't been right there to see it happen, and I think Jerry Krohl was as shocked as I was.

"What's this Western something or other cost?" Grandfather asked.

"Western Power and Light?" Krohl said. "I'll see where it closed today."

He came back and said twenty-two and three-eighths, and grandfather said he'd take ten shares, just to try it out, and he sat down to write out a check.

That got him into a discussion about brokerage commissions and something called odd lots, and a few other complications about buying stock that he might have learned himself if he'd read the stuff that Krohl sent to him. At one point I thought he was going to say it wasn't worth the trouble, and walk out, but finally he agreed that Krohl should buy the stock and send him the bill.

"Do you want us to mail your stock certificate to you?" Krohl asked.

"Suit yourself," Grandfather said.

"I mean, do you want to hold the certificate yourself, or should we hold it for you?"

Grandfather wanted to know what difference it made.

"No difference," Krohl said. "It's just a matter of convenience. If this is something you're going to hang onto for a long time, you might prefer to have the certificate. If you think you might sell it soon, it might be better to have us hold it for you, because it will save you the trouble of returning it when you sell."

"What does Pilkins do?" Grandfather asked.

"Oh, he holds his own certificates."

"I don't see any point in buying something and then selling it right away," Grandfather said. "And anyway, I'd like to see what it is I've bought."

Krohl said that was probably a good idea and he'd buy the stock first thing in the morning—"At the market."

"What does that mean?" Grandfather asked which started another involved discussion. They got everything arranged, and then Grandfather had a last minute doubt or two and got to wondering if maybe he shouldn't think it over some more.

"Let's do it this way," Krohl said. "If you change your mind, telephone. If I haven't heard from you by noon tomorrow, I'll place your order."

Grandfather maybe would have rather had it the other way around, but finally he agreed.

"I was talking with the sheriff this morning," Krohl said. "He tells me you don't think this Mark Vaughan murdered Professor Pesman."

"Maybe he did, and maybe he didn't," Grandfather said. "Pilkins has a mind like a one-way street with no exits. Once he gets an idea, he won't let go of it until he's ridden it clear to the end, and even then it takes something of the nature of an earthquake to disengage him. Right now the circumstances don't favor Vaughan, but I figure the sheriff is a long way from proving his case."

Krohl said he thought the sheriff was still investigating, and Grandfather said the sheriff wasn't trying to find out anything, he was just trying to prove something, which was an entirely different kind of investigation.

"By the way," Grandfather said, "did you ever get permission to sell the professor's stock?"

"No," Krohl said. "But I did it anyway."

"You didn't!" Grandfather said. He stared at Krohl, and then he started to laugh. "I'd like to see Junior Temple's face when he hears about that!"

"He'll faint, probably," Krohl said. "How was it he put it to me? 'No authority, no right, no business—' Baloney! I talked to my own lawyer, whose name doesn't happen to be Temple. Junior's right when he says he has no authority, but a named executor who's worth his salt will take any necessary steps to preserve the estate. I've committed an illegal act, but my act saved the estate some twelve thousand dollars and possibly a whole lot more. The proceeds of the sale are in Pesman's brokerage account, waiting for the executor to take over. If the Probate court takes any notice of my action at all, it will be to congratulate me."

"It doesn't stand to reason that they would penalize a man for saving that much money," Grandfather said. "The heir should be grateful to you."

"I hope he is. I'd like to have him for a client. What happens to the estate if it turns out that Vaughan did do it?"

"I haven't any idea," Grandfather said. "Ask Junior Temple."

"No thanks. That's the last place I'd go for legal information."

"Did either of the Temples ever buy any stock?"

"Not from me," Krohl said.

Everyone else had left, and I managed to remind Grandfather that it was five o'clock, and we'd originally came to town to do some eating. Krohl had been talking just to be polite, because he got his hat and left with us, locking up on the way out.

I tried to steer Grandfather into a stylish restaurant down the street.

"That looks too expensive," he said.

"How about buying me a steak dinner with all those stock dividends you're going to get?" I asked.

We ate hamburgers and chili at the diner around the corner, and Grandfather rushed me through the meal because he had a sudden urge to talk with Lyle Jones again.

There is this to say about a cow barn: it always smells the same, and if there are any commercial possibilities in that smell I haven't been able to think of them. We caught Mr. Jones overseeing his milking machines again, and he let me do some of the work for him while he talked with Grandfather. Attaching a milking machine is no more trouble than attaching a hose to a faucet, even if there are four connections to make instead of one. My main trouble was that I didn't know the social standing of the various cows. Mr. Jones seemed to think that if a cow got milked out of turn it would cause all kinds of bickering and jealousy in the herd.

What Grandfather wanted from Mr. Jones was a detailed account of his activity on the afternoon Professor Pesman was murdered. He didn't come right out and ask him, of course. He started in by asking if he'd seen anything suspicious that afternoon. Mr. Jones upset the whole line of questioning by saying that the sheriff had already asked him that, and he couldn't possibly have seen anything suspicious because he was planting soybeans over on the south forty, which was as far as he could get from the Courthouse without using a road or trespassing.

"The sheriff's asked everyone else around here, too," he said. "Nobody saw nothing. You're just wasting your time."

"That may be," Grandfather said, "but when I waste my time I like to get my money's worth." And before Mr. Jones could figure that one out, he aimed a few more questions at him.

It was the most wasteful money's worth Grandfather ever got anywhere. All of his questions hit that south forty and stuck there. Mr. Jones had spend the afternoon in his south forty, from which he could see neither the Courthouse nor the highway, and he was so busy he wouldn't have been looking if he could have seen them. He also didn't seem to care. I had the impression that Mr. Jones wouldn't have gone to see that murder even if he'd known when and where it would happen.

At seven o'clock we were back at Professor Alford's house. The professor wasn't home yet, but Mrs. Alford let us wait, and it was a long wait. I went over to a bookcase to look for something to read, and the books were all in foreign languages. Grandfather picked up a paper to read, found it was the Wiston paper, and put it down again. Mrs. Alford came in and tried to make conversation, but Grandfather doesn't think too much of women as conversationalists, and he may have let it show. After about three passes she excused herself, but she didn't take it personally, because about eight o'clock she brought in coffee for Grandfather, and chocolate milk for me, and a plate of cookies.

It was nearly nine when Professor Alford came in. He has always made me think psychology might be a pretty good business to be in, because I never saw him when he wasn't cheerful and ready to crack a joke. "Rastin!" he said. "It's been a quiet night. What ill wind deposited you here?"

Mrs. Alford explained that we'd been waiting she didn't know how long—though I could have told her—and the professor said he was sorry, but he'd been at a little dinner party for Jim Collins, a Southern Ohio University professor who was visiting the campus.

"And now," he said, when he'd gotten himself settled in his favorite chair, and lit his pipe, and slipped off his shoes, "before we talk about whatever it is that's kept a restless old dog like you sitting here for hours, maybe you'll tell me why the devil you sicked the sheriff on me."

That made Grandfather blink. "Sicked the sheriff on *you*?"

"The day after Pesman was murdered, one of his deputies breezed in here and tied me up for two hours. Seems you convinced the sheriff that the one that killed Pesman had to know the maze, and there weren't many eligible, but I was extremely prominent among the ones that were. In fact, the deputy said you mentioned me by name."

"That's right," Grandfather said. "I did."

Professor Alford laughed his big, booming laugh. His round face crinkled up, and his stomach shook, and if he'd had a white beard instead of a little black goatee he could have passed for Santa Claus in street clothes.

"I ought to banish you," he said. "But I won't. I haven't had as much fun in years as I had with that deputy. I led him on, and kept changing the subject every time he asked for my alibi, and finally when I had to leave or be late for my class I told him I was lunching with several very respectable people at the critical time. I'll bet he kicked his dog when he got home."

"Or his wife," Grandfather said. "The respectable people you were lunching with didn't happen to be Dean Morris and Professor Collins, did they?"

"No. It was actually a psychology staff meeting, but we combine it with lunch. Now, then."

His pipe had gone out, and he got out a miniature flame thrower he used for a lighter and worked up a good smog for himself. "You were saying," he said, "or weren't you?"

"Not yet, but I will. I'm curious about this fellow Collins."

"That's an odd sentiment to have about Collins. He's about the most uncurious man I've ever met. He's a scientist, and a good one, and he seems to function like a very precise piece of machinery."

"Dean Morris told me how he happened to be here," Grandfather said. "I want to know just two things about him. Had he ever heard of Charlie Pesman before he came here, and was his coming here really your idea, or was it his."

Professor Alford smoked for awhile, and then he stopped smoking and let his pipe go out, and then he had to light it again. "You ask the quaintest questions," he said finally. "I'd like to see you on the committee that administers oral exams to graduate students."

"Maybe some other time," Grandfather said. "Right now those two questions are the only ones I want to talk about."

"All right. The answer to both of them is—I don't know. We talked about Pesman in Chicago—you knew I met Collins in Chicago—but I *think* I was the one responsible. I've always enjoyed talking about Pesman, poor fellow. He was such a wonderful subject for conversation, especially with a stranger who'd never heard of him. Yet we talked about so many things, and the conversation splashed around so untidily—and so did the drinks, that evening—that I simply do not remember. The same applies to question number two. Sometime during the evening he mentioned that he was making a change, and I told him about the opening here, but whether he suggested that he might be interested, or whether I asked him if he were interested, I couldn't say. I don't suppose that helps you."

"I don't suppose," Grandfather said. "But thanks anyway. Now I want to go home, where I can do some thinking."

"Surely you don't have to rush off," Professor Alford said. "Can't you stay long enough to tell me why all this interest in Collins?"

"Some other time," Grandfather said.

"One of these days I'm going to strap you to that rocking chair of yours, and perform a few psychological tests."

Before we got to the door Mrs. Alford came in with refreshments, and then of course there had to be more talk, but after another twenty minutes or so we did get away. It had been a long day, and we were both pretty tired, and I thought Grandfather was in a hurry to get home.

So I tried a joke on him, which is seldom a safe thing to do. "I suppose you'll want to stop and talk to Nat Barlow," I said.

"Nat will be in bed by this time," Grandfather said.

"Willie, then. You should have a lot of questions for Willie. Those two are the only ones you haven't talked to yet."

"Have you got a flashlight?" Grandfather asked.

"In the glove compartment. Why?"

"I would like to stop at the Courthouse."

"Professor Alford must have put something in your coffee," I said. "I suppose the flashlight's good for the third degree, but how are you going to go about probing Willie's subconscious when all you can get are yes and no answers?"

"I don't want to question Willie," Grandfather said. "I want another look at the maze."

CHAPTER XII

Professor Pesman's maze was a disagreeable place to be in the day time. At night it was downright frightening, and I didn't like it. I followed Grandfather over the gate and kept close behind him while he went to work with my flashlight, and if you'd seen him moving along at a squat and flashing that light around on the path you'd have thought he'd lost his last penny when he was there before, and was looking for it.

We moved on into the maze, following the tape Sheriff Pilkins had left there, and that tape was the only white thing around at night. The sky was overcast, and once we got into the maze we couldn't even see the lights from the occasional car that went past on the highway. There weren't any lights on in the Courthouse, and if there had been they wouldn't have helped us.

I thought about Professor Collins, lost in there after dark, and felt sympathetic towards him. I didn't blame him for running off at the first opportunity without saying thank you for a ham sandwich. If Professor Pesman hadn't already been dead, Collins would have had good reason to sue him.

Grandfather moved in spurts—a few steps forward, then a squatting meditation with the flashlight, then a few more steps forward. The novelty of this wore off, after a time, and I began to feel impatient. Sheriff Pilkins and half a dozen men hadn't found anything in broad daylight, so it seemed ridiculous for Grandfather to think he could find something at night with a flashlight. I told him so, and he said if I didn't like it I could go back and wait in the car. That didn't strike me as being any more interesting than watching Grandfather play with the flashlight, so I stayed.

I don't know how long it took us to reach the place where Professor Pesman was murdered. I wasn't wearing my watch that day, and when Grandfather has a job on his hands, the last thing he is ever interested in is the time. He wouldn't even talk to me, though once in a while he would mutter something to himself. By the time we eventually did get to the place where the professor's body was found, I'd begun to worry about the flashlight batteries, which were not as fresh as I would like batteries to be when I explore a maze at night.

Grandfather straightened up, and said, "All right. We can go home now."

"There's a lot of maze left," I said. "Why don't you look around until the batteries burn out? I'm in no hurry. Probably a person hasn't really lived until he's tried to find his way out of here in the dark."

"What would be hard about that?" Grandfather asked. "All we have to do would be take a hold of this tape and follow it. Here—I'll show you."

He picked up the tape, and switched off the flashlight, and ten seconds later that bad joke of mine saved Grandfather's life, and probably mine too. We hadn't taken more than a couple of steps when a gun went off right up ahead of us where the path turned.

Grandfather jerked me back against the hedge, and there were two more shots, the second plowing into the path by my foot. I was too paralyzed to move, but Grandfather kept a grip on my arm, and I could feel his muscles tensed for action in case this gunman came within reach. Grandfather was Borgville's blacksmith when he was a young man, and he still looks it. He's always said he'd be a match for any man half his age, which I never doubted, and that gunman would have been in for a surprise of his life if he'd come forward to gloat over our dead bodies. He didn't though. He was playing it cautious, or maybe the maze had him scared, too.

The night was absolutely still, without even a whisper of a breeze, and I was certain my breathing could be heard for half a mile. Then a car came along the highway, and Grandfather gave me a push, and with that little noise to cover us we edged backwards a few steps, keeping close to the hedge. Another car came, and we made a few more steps. Then there was another shot that snapped past my ear and hit the fence in the hedge, and went whining away somewhere.

Grandfather cupped his hand to my ear, and whispered, "Get ready." Then he stooped low for a moment. He got a handful of gravel, and when the next car came he threw the gravel and we tore around the corner and into the next alley. He pulled me down, and we both stretched out flat, with me hanging onto a couple of handfuls of gravel for dear life, while the gunman went wild. He emptied his gun, reloaded, and emptied it a second time. One shot tugged at my pant leg, but the others were all over the maze.

A moment of silence followed. Then we heard one more shot, and the gravel crunching as the gunman ran away.

"I hope he gets lost in the maze," I muttered.

Grandfather hushed me, and whispered that it might be a trick. We lay there on the gravel straining our ears, while footsteps grew fainter and fainter and finally we couldn't hear them anymore.

"What do we do?" I asked. "Wait here until morning?"

For a second I thought I heard the gunman coming back, but it was only Grandfather scratching his head. "This is the silliest thing I've ever done," he announced.

"Well, do something bright, and get us out of here," I said. "And the next time you get me into a gun battle, I want something to shoot back with, and something more solid than a hedge to hide behind."

"Just a moment. I want to patch up my arm."

"You mean you're hit?"

I forgot all about the gunman, and grabbed the flashlight and turned it on. Grandfather's red shirt sleeve was stained a darker red. I tried to rip the sleeve off, but it wouldn't rip, so I made him take the shirt off. Grandfather told me to turn the light off, because he was only grazed anyway, but he had an ugly gash in his arm. I was all set to bandage it with my handkerchief, but he wouldn't let me. He said he'd noticed the condition my handkerchiefs were usually in, and he didn't know of a more certain way to get lockjaw. Then I tried to rip a piece out of his shirttail, and he wouldn't let me do that, either, because it was his favorite shirt. Finally I sacrificed my shirt, which wasn't so hard to tear, and then we turned off the light and sat down to listen for footsteps.

Grandfather didn't wait patiently. He kept twisting around, and muttering about what a fool he'd been, and finally he announced that the gunman would be an even bigger fool if he wasn't miles away from there at that minute.

"I heard a car start up a little while back," he said. "It probably was him leaving, and if he has any sense he's in Wiston arranging an alibi right now. Let's get going."

"Suit yourself," I said. "We can't any more than get shot, and that might be better than having to spend the night here."

We found the tape and started following it, not using the flashlight, and just around the first turn Grandfather stopped so suddenly that I ran into him.

"You didn't signal," I said. "What's the matter?"

"He's cut the tape," Grandfather said, "and taken it with him. Looks like we're stuck here after all."

"Then we have two choices," I said. "We can try to find our way out, and probably get so lost that the professor himself wouldn't have been able to find us, or we can sit down and starve to death while we wait for someone to think of looking for us in here."

"With your car parked on the highway, it won't take them long to get the idea."

"Supposing the gunman ran off with my car?" I said.

"Don't tell me you were idiot enough to leave your keys!"

"No," I said. "But there are ways of starting a car without keys."

"Even so, I think we'd better wait here."

"I vote for trying to find our way out. We won't, but it'll give us something to do."

Grandfather grabbed my arm. "Someone's coming," he whispered.

We backed up against the hedge. The footsteps came on slowly, passed by the opening into our alley, and then came back. Grandfather grabbed, timing it perfectly, and a voice let out a very startled, "Uh!"

It was Willie.

I was all for getting out to my car and heading for a doctor, to get Grandfather's arm looked at properly, but Grandfather said that when an innocent citizen is shot at he should tell the law about it, even if the enforcement officer is afflicted with rigor mortis above his shoulders. Willie had us out of the maze in about seven minutes. I followed along through all those twists and turns wondering how he did it—he must have had the thing memorized right down to the last leaf on every hedge, and he did it without a flashlight too.

Once in the Courthouse I went down to the little room Sheriff Pilkins had used the night the professor was murdered, and got the rocking chair for Grandfather, and then I left Willie in charge of him while I went to telephone.

First I called the operator and told her there was an emergency at the Courthouse, and we needed a doctor, and then I tried to call Sheriff Pilkins at home. His wife said he'd had a report of shooting at the Courthouse, and maybe I could get a hold of him there, if it was something important. I told her I was calling from the Courthouse, and right away she wanted to know all about it. I had some trouble hanging up on her without making it sound impolite.

Willie had gone to work on Grandfather's arm, which was still bleeding. He brought out a first aid kit, and put on a bandage that looked like a bandage ought to look. He did such a good job of it that Grandfather began to wonder if the doctor wouldn't be an unnecessary expense. "All he'll do is take the bandage off and put another one on," he said.

Before we could get that worked into a proper kind of argument a horn started blasting away out at the gate, and Willie went to let the sheriff in.

He came charging into the house with his gun in his hand, all set to take on a whole gang of desperados, and it was probably the biggest anti-climax of his career when he found no one there but Grandfather and me.

"Why don't you two stay home?" he roared.

"With the kind of law enforcement we have in this county," Grandfather said, "one place is about as dangerous as another."

"Who shot you?"

"The same person that murdered Professor Pesman," Grandfather said.

"Nonsense. He's in jail in Wiston."

"Didn't they tell you?" Grandfather said. "He escaped this evening."

That seemed about as bad as any joke I'd ever heard, and I don't think anyone but the sheriff would have fallen for it. But Sheriff Pilkins tends to get emotionally upset whenever he happens onto Grandfather unexpectedly, and anyway, he'd been awakened out of a sound sleep by a wild telephone call and his thinking was fuzzier than usual. He had to telephone the county jail and have someone go down and look at Mark Vaughan, just to make sure he was still there. Even then he didn't suspect it was a joke.

"You're crazy," he said. "Vaughan didn't escape."

"You don't say," Grandfather said. "I'm sorry to hear that."

"Why?"

"Because it was the murderer who shot up the maze, tonight, and if Vaughan has been in jail all evening he can't be the murderer."

"How do you know it was the murderer doing the shooting?"

"It's just as sound a guess as yours is that Vaughan is the murderer. Who told you about the shooting?"

"Some hysterical female telephoned and said she'd been driving by here and heard shots."

The sheriff got two of his deputies out of bed and told them to come over and help out, and then he wanted to hear all about what had happened. Grandfather told him everything except why we were in the maze in the first place, and later, when the doctor had shooed us out of the room, he tried to get information from me and got mad when I couldn't tell him.

"Your Grandfather's mind is failing him in his old age," he said. "What the devil could he find in there at night?"

"He found the murderer," I said, "and that's better than you've done."

Sheriff Pilkins started to explain very patiently that he'd already found the murderer, and then he decided it wasn't worth the trouble. When his deputies came he sent them out to have a look at the scene of the shooting, and of course Willie had to go along to guide them, and put the tape back if he could find it.

The sheriff wanted to start in on Grandfather again as soon as the doctor left, but Grandfather had been ordered home to bed, and that was one order he intended to take.

"I've done as much of your work as I'm going to do for one day," he said.

"I'll see you first thing in the morning, then," the sheriff said.

"Not unless you telephone first for an appointment," Grandfather said.

Willie guided us through the maze out to my car and the two of us went home.

I will say this for Mom. She realized that what had happened was over with, so she did not throw a tantrum all over the living room floor when we walked in. She didn't even ask questions, other than to find out if we were hungry. Grandfather gave her a fast summary, and she said the rest could wait until morning, and hurried us off to bed. I thought I saw a quiet glint in her eyes, though, and I wouldn't be surprised if she waylaid Grandfather later on to tell him that if he insisted on getting in gun battles he should get himself a proper bodyguard and leave me at home.

We both slept late, but when I woke up Doc Beyers was already there to see Grandfather. Grandfather had called him as soon as he got out of bed, because he had very little confidence in any doctor who would live in Wiston. When I went in to say good morning he was sitting up in his rocking chair with his arm in a sling, eating breakfast, and if he had lost much blood the night before it hadn't affected his appetite.

"Did Sheriff Pilkins call?" I asked.

"Three times," Grandfather said.

"I don't suppose he caught our gunman."

Grandfather snorted. "If he'd managed anything that sensational, do you suppose he'd bothered to call me?"

I didn't suppose so, and I went downstairs to have my breakfast so I wouldn't miss anything when the sheriff got there.

Sheriff Pilkins was in one of his thoughtful moods that morning. He went upstairs quietly, and he even took the trouble to ask Grandfather how he felt before he accepted the chair I brought in for him. Grandfather said later that a lack of sleep sometimes affected him that way, but I wondered if maybe he'd suddenly realized that he could easily have had two more murders to investigate that morning, namely Grandfather's and mine, and the idea scared him.

"All we found was a lot of hardware lying around, and we recovered one of the slugs," he said. "If we ever find the gun we won't have any trouble proving it shot at you. Also, we know the guy doesn't carry a knife, because he shot a hole in the tape in order to break it. But that's all we know. I've located three people who drove by while you were in the maze, and they remember seeing one car parked there. None of them saw anyone on foot. Maybe the guy flew in."

"He didn't fly out," Grandfather said. "Any news from Ohio?"

"Boy telephoned last evening. Didn't I tell you?"

"Would I be asking you if you had?"

"I guess not. Well, you were right. This Professor Collins was one of the investors in Pesman's Modern Merchandising Corporation. There were five others, including Pesman himself. Vaughan—the old man—put up twenty-five thousand. The others put up five. Pesman was going to develop some revolutionary advertising techniques based upon sound psychology, whatever that means. He expected to make a billion dollars, and all the stockholders expected to become millionaires. Then he piddled away the money in far-fetched research projects. Vaughan and a couple of the others contributed more money which went the same way. Finally the corporation got buried during the Depression."

"Interesting," Grandfather said. "Whatever else Collins may be, there's no doubt about his being a liar."

"He is that," the sheriff agreed, "but it's not much of a basis for an arrest. To continue—the stockholders who lost their money hounded Pesman mercilessly. Everyone except Vaughan, that is. Vaughan was sure Pesman would eventually make good the loss, and he believed it to his dying day, or at least he said he did. The others were bitter, but there wasn't anything they could do about it. They didn't know Pesman inherited a fortune. They did hear that he was living near Wiston, Michigan, but none of them attached any special significance to it. They thought he was all but broke when he left Southern Ohio University."

"Then Collins attended some special kind of meeting in Chicago, and met Alford, and came home with the information that Pesman was now very rich. The four of them held a meeting. They didn't know Vaughan was dead, but they wouldn't have invited him anyway, because he could see no wrong in Pesman. They figured that Pesman had finally cashed in on the ideas he'd developed at their expense, and made a lot of money, and they didn't like that. Collins offered to look into it if they'd contribute a bit towards his expenses, which they did. Now the other three are mad at Collins, because as we know he got himself invited here by Wiston College, so the college also paid his expenses. For all his distinguished professional reputation, he seems to be something of a heel. Which is irrelevant as far as Pesman's murder is concerned."

"It explains Pesman's will," Grandfather said. "The others hounded Pesman, and Pesman figured it maybe wasn't his fault the Depression came along when it did. Vaughan was decent about it, so he, or rather his son, gets the money."

"Anyway, this clears up a few things for us without really explaining anything. We know why Collins came to Wiston, and we know why he happened to get lost in the maze—he was probably trying to get in to see the professor. But we also know that Collins isn't the murderer."

"It *was* him that hailed the professor in Wiston, though," Grandfather said. "The professor figured Collins would be pestering him, so he ordered the gate kept locked. He just didn't want to talk with the guy. Have you checked to see where Collins was last night?"

"He attended some kind of dinner party, and then he went back to his motel, and stayed there. Or so he says. I have a man working on it."

"Not Steve Carling, I hope."

"Look," the sheriff said. "I have an idea. We know Collins didn't murder the professor, but supposing he convinced Mark Vaughan that he had a scheme that would recover some of his father's money, and brought him up here to help out. The two of them could have hatched out a plan together, and then Vaughan got into a squabble with the professor and killed him. Naturally that wasn't part of the plan, and Collins didn't know about it when he got lost in the maze. He was still working on the plan. It seems just possible, to me."

"It doesn't to me," Grandfather said.

The sheriff ignored him. "I don't know if it would make Collins an accessory to the murder—I'll have to take it up with the County Attorney. Since we know as much as we do, we might be able to get the whole story out of Collins. With Collins as a witness I'd say we'd have a good case against Vaughan."

Grandfather rocked a little faster, and didn't say anything.

"Well, I have plenty to do, so I guess I'll be going."

But for once he didn't rush off. He asked Grandfather again how the arm was feeling, and said he'd look in on him soon and he'd let him know if anything important happened. I went to the front door with him, and then I hurried back upstairs.

"What do you think of the sheriff's idea?" I said.

"Two things happened," Grandfather said. "The professor got murdered, and we got shot at. Pilkins can't see any connection between them, mainly because he has Vaughan in jail where he couldn't have done the shooting." He rocked for a while, and then he said, "Johnny, why would anyone want to shoot us?"

"Maybe there *was* something lost in the maze," I said, "and the murderer was afraid we'd find it."

"Ah!" Grandfather said. "I'd forgotten. There was something lost in the maze, and I *did* find it."

"You found it? Then—"

"Johnny," Grandfather said, "Pilkins is the sort of person who'd hang a picture of a waterfall upside down, and claim it proved water could flow uphill."

CHAPTER XIII

Saturday and Sunday Grandfather was convalescing, and as far as I know the sheriff was, too. He telephoned once, to tell Grandfather that Professor Collins had been in to notify him that he was leaving town Sunday night. The sheriff gave Collins a good going over about all the lies he'd told, and tried to get him to admit that he'd been up to something with Vaughan, but Collins said he'd never seen Vaughan before, and when the sheriff hauled him over to the jail Vaughan said he'd never seen Collins before, and that was that.

The sheriff would like to have arrested him, if only on general principles, but he couldn't think of a charge. He wanted to know if Grandfather had anything in mind, because Collins had already turned down the Wiston College job, and once he got over the state line it would take more than a polite invitation to get him back to Michigan.

"Try trespassing," Grandfather said.

"With those signs out there inviting him in?"

"He wasn't a salesman," Grandfather said. "The signs didn't say, 'College Professors Welcome.'"

"But Pesman is dead. Who'd sign the complaint?"

Grandfather chuckled. "Try Junior Temple."

That was where Sheriff Pilkins hung up on him, and Professor Collins left Wiston Sunday night without any special ceremony, unless Wiston College gave him a farewell dinner, which I doubt.

Monday morning Grandfather took his arm out of the sling, and put on his red shirt, which Mom had washed and patched with a piece of shirt tail, and we all went over to Wiston to see Mark Vaughan's preliminary hearing.

Justice Frazier's Justice Court wasn't designed for a large crowd. It wasn't designed to hold any more people than the average family living room holds, because that's what it was—Ted Frazier's living room. There wasn't even elbow room for the witnesses, let alone the people who wanted to watch, so Ted moved everyone downstairs to his recreation room and sent out for a load of chairs.

We finally got settled there. Old Man Temple sat at a card table with Mark Vaughan, and Junior Temple fluttered around at the back of the room, ready to run errands in case any turned up that needed running. The County Attorney, Mr. Hocking, was at another card table with one of his assistants, looking bored with the proceedings even before they started. He had a little mustache that he liked to call everyone's attention to by playing with it. Sheriff Pilkins was present with two of his deputies, to see how Mr. Hocking made out with the evidence he'd collected, and everyone who'd worked for the professor was there—everyone except Willie, who for obvious reasons wasn't considered good witness material.

Justice Frazier took a seat behind an old mahogany table that made a wonderful racket when he rapped on it, and got things started. The Justice was a pleasant young man about thirty, and he was popular even with the defendants in his court because he ran things as if he knew what he was doing, and enjoyed it, but hadn't anything personal against them for all that.

Now as I understand it, a preliminary hearing is usually pretty much of a cut and dried procedure. The prosecution has to show the court that there is enough evidence to justify holding the defendant for trial, and when it's done that the hearing is over.

But there wasn't anything slipshod about the way the County Attorney Hocking went about showing probable cause of guilt. He'd heard that Old Man Temple had a few tricks up his sleeve, and he wasn't taking any chances. He was no fool, either. He'd figured out the gimmick about the bell ringing when anyone entered the maze, or someone in his office had, and he was certainly prepared to make something of it.

There were the usual preliminaries, with Doc Phillips testifying about how and when and where the professor got killed, and one of the deputies making a mess of trying to explain the maze, and then Mr. Hocking began to pile on the witnesses.

First came Pete Kruger and Nat Barlow, to testify that the gate had been locked, and that they'd worked in the Courthouse yard all afternoon, so the murderer couldn't have come in that way. Then came Ed Fellows, to tell what time he'd seen Vaughan entering the maze, and there was Ed and Sam Baker, and Mr. Crabtree to tell about what time he came out, and what had been said.

Then Mr. Hocking called Mrs. Glover. She had a lot less trouble remembering about the bell than she had when Grandfather talked to her. Then she said if it rang more than once she hadn't noticed it, but now she was certain that the only time it rang was just before two o'clock, when Vaughan had entered the maze.

Mr. Boyd was called to explain how the bell worked, and then Mr. Hocking actually called Old Man Temple to the stand, to tell about the professor's will, so the court would know why Vaughan had murdered the professor. Mr. Temple was a very good witness. He answered all the questions without beating around the bush at all, and it looked to me as if Mark Vaughan was going to be a guest of Borg County for a long time, or at least until someone got around to holding a trial for him.

I don't know how Mr. Vaughan was taking all this, because he sat with his back to me, but none of it seemed to be disturbing Old Man Temple. He didn't interrupt Mr. Hocking once, and he didn't even bother to question the witnesses. He just sat there mostly with a grin on his face, but it wasn't clear whether he was grinning about something that was happening, or something that was going to happen.

Mr. Hocking wound things up with a flourish, having proved beyond a doubt that Mark Vaughan was the only one who could have been in the maze when Professor Pesman was murdered, and that he was the only person who had any reason to want the job done. He sat down with a look of smug satisfaction on his face, as if to say—what more probable cause do you want?

Old Man Temple got up. There was a little sparring with Justice Frazier over some point of law that I didn't understand. I think maybe Mr. Temple wanted him to call the whole thing off right then, but Ted Frazier was enjoying himself too much, and he wouldn't do it.

Mr. Temple called Grandfather as his first witness.

"Mr. Rastin," he said, "where were you on the night of Thursday, June 20th between the hours of ten o'clock and midnight?"

"I was in Charlie Pesman's maze most of that time," Grandfather said, "with my grandson."

"Why were you in the maze?"

"I went there to look for evidence that would help prove who killed Pesman."

"Did anything unusual happen while you were there?"

"I got shot."

"Did you see who shot you?"

"No."

"Do you know who shot you?"

"Yes."

"Who, then?"

"Charlie Pesman's murderer," Grandfather said.

Mr. Hocking objected all over the place and Grandfather had to admit that he had no proof that it was the murderer who shot him.

"Why do you think it was the murderer?" Mr. Temple asked.

"Who but the murderer would want to keep me from finding evidence?"

"Could it have been Mark Vaughan who shot you?"

"The sheriff told me Vaughan was in jail that night."

"Thank you," Mr. Temple said.

Then Mr. Temple called the sheriff, to prove that Mr. Vaughan had been in jail that night.

Ted Frazier looked puzzled, and Mr. Hocking said, "I hope you don't think this proves anything."

"Now, Sid," Old Man Temple said, "I've taught you one or two of the maybe three or four things you know, and if you'll sit tight and listen I might be able to teach you something else."

Everyone laughed, and Mr. Hocking sat down looking disgusted.

Mr. Temple called his next witness, a Mrs. Penelope Jackson, who said she was a housewife and looked it. "Did you see the defendant at any time on Tuesday, June 11th?" he asked.

"Yes," she said. "He called at my home that day and sold me a set of encyclopedias."

"Where is your home?"

"In Camboy. It's a little town southeast of Benton Harbor."

"How far is that from Wiston?"

"It's more than a hundred miles. How much depends on what way you come."

"The way you came, how long did it take?"

"Two hours and a half, and we hurried."

"Fine. Tell me, Mrs. Jackson—what time was it that Mark Vaughan left your home that day?"

"Right around eleven thirty. In the morning."

"Thank you," Mr. Temple said.

Mr. Hocking started to stand up when that critical question was asked. And when Mrs. Jackson said eleven thirty he sat down again and laughed.

Ted Frazier rapped for order.

The next witness was Mabel Seacomb, who said she ran a diner on Highway 60 east of Three Rivers. "Did you see the defendant at any time on Tuesday, June 11th?" Mr. Temple asked her.

"Yes, I did," she said. "He ate lunch at my diner. I particularly remember him because he was in such a hurry. He wanted food that didn't take long to fix."

"And what time did the defendant Mark Vaughan leave your diner?"

"At exactly twelve thirty."

"How does it happen that you can be so precise about the time?" Mr. Temple asked.

"Well, as he was going out, he bumped into Fred Hobbs, who was coming in. They collided, and then they both laughed and apologized, and then this Mr. Vaughan went ahead and left. And Fred comes into my diner every day at twelve-thirty, right on the button. He hasn't missed it by a minute in five years."

"You're positive he didn't miss it by a minute on June 11th?"

"I sure am. When Fred comes in I always look up at the clock—to see if it's right, you know."

"Thank you," Mr. Temple said.

"For God's sake!" Mr. Hocking said. "Are we going to have to sit here all day listening to irrelevancies like this?"

That started a hot argument, Mr. Hocking claiming that where Vaughan was at eleven thirty or twelve thirty had nothing to do with the case unless it proved he couldn't have been at the Courthouse between one forty-five and three. "All Temple has shown so far is that Vaughan was on his way there," he said.

"My intention," Mr. Temple said, "is to show conclusively that Mark Vaughan could not have been at the Courthouse on Tuesday, June 11th, at any time *except* between one forty-five and three."

"Who's saying he was?" Mr. Hocking wanted to know.

Ted Frazier rapped for order, and nodded to Mr. Temple to continue.

Mr. Temple then called a Mrs. Ruth Emery, a housewife who also looked it, and she said that Mr. Vaughan had called on her at her home in Alcanna between five thirty and six o'clock the evening of June 11th, to try to sell her a set of encyclopedias, and if he'd been in Wiston at three o'clock he must have driven awfully fast getting to Alcanna, because it had taken her a lot longer than that. She hadn't bought the encyclopedias, and she would have liked to tell us why, but Mr. Temple wouldn't let her.

There was also a waitress who'd served a late supper to Mr. Vaughan at a restaurant in Alcanna, and the woman who owned the motel Mr. Vaughan had stayed in that night, and then Mr. Temple summed up for the court, saying that unless the prosecution was prepared to prove that Mark Vaughan was a practitioner of teleportation, he had shown that it was impossible for him to have been at the Courthouse at any time that day except when the Prosecution's witnesses said he was there.

Justice Frazier agreed that he had done that, though he didn't exactly understand why, and Mr. Hocking said, "Amen, and let's get out of here." It was after twelve o'clock, and everyone was getting restless.

"I have one more witness, Your Honor," Mr. Temple said.

Ted Frazier looked at his watch, for about the tenth time in the last five minutes, and said the court would hear the one witness.

"This witness," Mr. Temple said, "is known to many of those present as Willie, or Silly Willie. Bring the witness in, please."

Mr. Hocking was on his feet right away, with all kinds of objections. Willie couldn't be a witness, he said, and Justice Frazier wanted to know why.

"Because the guy can't talk!" Mr. Hocking said.

Justice Frazier considered this, and then he said that if the witness couldn't talk no doubt that would be brought out in his testimony, and bring on the witness. In the meantime Junior Temple had called Willie in from somewhere outside, and he hurried up to the front of the room, baggy pants and shirt flopping.

Mr. Hocking turned away, muttering something about how calling a witness who couldn't talk made a mockery of the proceedings, and Willie faced him and said, in a loud and clear voice, "Who says I can't talk?"

It caused a sensation.

Justice Frazier pounded his table a few times and then gave up, probably because he knew no one could hear his pounding. Things finally quieted down long enough for Mr. Temple to start asking questions, but they didn't stay quieted down long. Mr. Temple said, "Would you tell us your name?" And Willie said, "Wilhelminia Adel Davis."

"You mean he's a *girl*?" Mr. Hocking demanded, when he could make himself heard.

Willie looked icicles at him, and said, "I'm a *woman*!" which caused another uproar. A few minutes before this everyone had been impatient to leave, but now nothing short of an explosion could have cleared that courtroom.

"I understand," Mr. Temple said, "that you have a personal interest in these proceedings."

"I certainly do," Willie said. "Charles Pesman was my stepfather."

"I think everyone would like to know why you were pretending to be a mute male," Mr. Temple said. "Will you tell us why?"

"I'll be glad to, though it may take a long story," Willie said. No one seemed to mind that. "When I was a child," Willie said, "my mother was Charles Pesman's housekeeper, and later his wife. He was the kindest man I've ever known, and the year and a half I lived at the Courthouse was the happiest time of my childhood. Then mother took me away, and got a divorce, and because mother and Professor Pesman had quarreled so bitterly, we never heard from him after that and mother married again and never wanted me to so much as mention him. But I didn't forget him, and the simple little psychological experiments he'd shown me made such an impression on me that I was determined to be a psychologist myself. Three years ago this coming September I entered Holdon College to major in psychology.

"Is Holdon College in Ohio?" Mr. Temple asked.

"No sir, it's in Minnesota."

"I'm glad to hear that," Mr. Temple said. "Some of us were beginning to think that almost all colleges are in Ohio. Go on, please."

"Towards the end of my first year—that would be the spring of 1961— I was talking with my advisor, Professor Barkley, and I mentioned that my stepfather had been a psychologist. It developed that Professor Barkley knew Professor Pesman—knew a lot about him, at least, and had corresponded with him. I said I would love to see him again, but I was afraid that I wouldn't receive a cordial reception, because of the trouble he and mother had. Professor Barkley has a wonderful sense of humor, and he helped me to work up the character of Willie. He even called the dramatics teacher to coach me in the part, and he also had a diagram of Professor Pesman's maze, which I spent hours studying.

"When school was out he gave me a letter to Professor Pesman that said that for all my odd appearance and my inability to talk, I was an excellent laboratory assistant, and I needed a summer job. If Professor could use me, he recommended me highly. Professor Pesman didn't really need me, but he seemed happy to have someone around who knew something about psychology. It was an excellent thing for me, because Professor Pesman has—had—a wonderful library, and I was able to do a lot of basic experiments, and the money helped when I went back to college in the fall. I came again last year, and this is my third summer."

"Did Professor Pesman give you any reason to suspect that he knew who you were?"

"Yes and no. I'll always wonder. He'd called me Willie as a child and occasionally I would see him watching me with a smile on his face. I hope he did know. No one else seemed to suspect anything, which surprised me. That in itself was quite a lesson in psychology."

Mr. Boyd was sitting in front of me, and he said aloud, "When I think of some of the stories I've told Willie—"

"Tell us what happened the afternoon of the eleventh," Mr. Temple said.

"We had an early lunch that day, and since the professor hadn't given me any work to do I went back to my room to do some reading. I finished my book—oh, it must have been shortly after one thirty—and I took it back up to the laboratory and picked out another one."

"Did you know that the professor was doing a special experiment that afternoon, and had left instructions that he wasn't to be disturbed?"

"No. I went to my room directly from lunch, when he went upstairs with Mr. Krohl, so I didn't hear anything about the special experiment."

"Did you meet anyone on your way upstairs?"

"No. The only person around was Mrs. Glover, but she was in the kitchen, and I didn't look in there."

"Very well. Shortly after one thirty you went up to the laboratory. What happened then?"

"I had some trouble finding a book I wanted, and while I was looking for it the maze bell rang. Since no one else was around, I went up into the cupola to observe."

"You've done this often—the observing, I mean?"

"Quite often."

"And there was a regular procedure that you followed?"

"Yes. The specimen—or person in the maze—was observed with binoculars, and his route was traced on a diagram of the maze. The pertinent information was recorded on the sheet, such as the date, the times, and the name of the person if known."

Mr. Temple brought out one of those mimeographed maps of the maze. "Is this the sheet you used that day?"

"Yes, it is," Willie said.

"Very well. Who was the specimen whom you observed in the maze?"

"It was the defendant, Mark Vaughan."

The room was absolutely quiet, and Mr. Hocking didn't even seem to be breathing.

"Did you observe Mark Vaughan all the time that he was in the maze?"

"I was observing all the time that he was in the maze. I did not see him all that time, because hedges obstruct the view into some of the alleys. I'd say I was able to observe him from sixty to seventy per cent of the time."

"Will you describe his actions?"

"They were very much like the actions of any specimen who entered the maze unknowingly. He was more persistent than most, so he got further into the maze than most did. He made his decisions quickly, and he seldom reversed himself. At his point of furthest penetration he knelt down for a few minutes."

"Were you able to see what he was doing when he knelt down?"

"No. The action puzzled me. The time of furthest penetration, as you will see in the diagram, was eleven minutes after two, and he started back again at two fourteen."

"Then he was considerably longer finding his way out than he had been finding his way in."

"Yes. I was surprised that he did find his way out. He made some very bad mistakes, and at one point I was ready to go down and rescue him. I'd say he was extraordinarily lucky."

"Did you have the impression that he'd ever been in the maze before?"

"I had the impression that he'd never been in that maze, or any other maze, before."

"Do you offer that as an expert's opinion?"

"I do," Willie said.

"And you continued to observe Mr. Vaughan until he left the maze. Please go on."

"As he approached the exit, some men appeared there. As we know now, they were waiting for him. I had not noticed them previously, though of course I could not see much of the highway because of the hedge, and Mr. Vaughan's car was parked directly in front of the opening. As Mr. Vaughan came out of the maze the men waiting there laughed at him, and then one of them—the deputy sheriff, Steve Carling—talked with him for a time. Then he turned and went back into the maze. This surprised me very much."

"How long was he in the maze the second time?"

"About eight minutes. You can see his route in the diagram. He left the maze the second time at four minutes after three, and got into his car and drove away."

"At any time while you were observing did you see Professor Pesman in the maze?"

"No, I did not."

"If he had been there would you have seen him?"

"If he had been anywhere in the vicinity of the specimen I would have seen him. Unless—"

"Unless what?"

"Unless he was not—well, upright. Or unless he was standing motionless where one of the hedges would obstruct my view."

"At the point of furthest penetration for this specimen, could you have seen Professor Pesman?"

"I could have seen him unless he was standing up against the closest hedge, or unless he were lying down."

"Are you certain about that?"

"Yes."

"How can you be certain?"

"Because you and I conducted some tests to determine just what I was able to see."

"Now, then—if, at this point of furthest penetration, Mark Vaughan made any kind of unusual movement, if he had struck a blow, for example, could you have seen him?"

"I could have seen him if he'd done it standing. I believe I would have seen him if he'd raised an arm while kneeling."

"Did you see him make such a movement?"

"I did not."

"I have here," Mr. Temple said, "a photographic enlargement of the maze diagram, and on this photograph I have placed the letters, X and Y. Does one of these letters mark the point of furthest penetration?"

"The letter Y," Willie said.

"Now if you will step down for a moment, Miss Davis, I'd like to have Evan Boyd take a look at this photograph."

Mr. Boyd went, and looked, and said yes, he knew where those two places were in the maze.

"Tell us about them." Mr. Temple said.

"Point Y is where Professor Pesman's body was found. And point X is where that fence post is—the place the doctors said the professor was murdered."

"Thank you," Mr. Temple said. "Now, Miss Davis—"

Willie went back to the witness chair.

"Did Mr. Vaughan, at any time while he was in the maze, approach point X?"

"No," Willie said. "Point X is a short distance beyond the point of furthest penetration. He never went past point Y."

"Is there any possible way he could have gone beyond point Y without your seeing him?"

"No, sir. He would have had to turn here—" She pointed. "—and that whole alley is visible from the cupola."

"Then if Professor Pesman was murdered at point X and if Vaughan never went near point X—"

"Objection!" Mr. Hocking yelled.

Justice Frazier hushed him. "May I see the photograph?" he asked.

Mr. Temple gave it to him and Mr. Hocking went up to see it for himself. He was no longer looking smug. He looked, in fact, like a man about to have a tooth pulled.

"Could you have seen the professor if he'd been at point X?" he asked Willie.

"There's a clear east-west view there," Willie said. "I could have seen him even if he'd been lying on the ground."

Mr. Hocking nodded, and went back to his chair.

"Your honor," Mr. Temple said, "we have established that the defendant could not have been in the maze at any time except the period between one forty-five—actually one forty-six, as this record proves—and four minutes after three. During that period he was under direct observation for from sixty to seventy per cent of the time. He did not meet the professor in the maze. He did not even approach the place where the crime occurred. He did find the professor's body where the murderer left it at point Y, and he reported that fact to the first people he met. Bill Rastin's experience suggests strongly that the murderer not only remains at large, but is highly dangerous. I submit that there is not probably cause that the defendant committed the crime."

Justice Frazier asked Mr. Hocking if he wanted to ask Willie any questions. The sheriff elbowed his way up front and whispered to Mr. Hocking, and then Mr. Hocking went up and asked Willie why she'd lied to the sheriff.

"I did tell one lie," she said. "At least, I shook my head when I should have nodded yes. That was when he asked me if I'd ever seen Mark Vaughan before. I was still very confused at the time, and was trying to decide whether I should keep being Willie, or start being myself again, and I just didn't know what to do. I wasn't aware of how important the question was, either. Then when Mr. Vaughan was charged with murder I went to Mr. Temple and told him, and Mr. Temple thought it would be best for me to wait and give my testimony at this hearing."

"He would," Mr. Hocking said.

"I'm sorry, Sheriff Pilkins," Willie said. "And I do apologize."

The sheriff's face turned moderately pink, but that time I think he was blushing.

"Anything else?" Justice Frazier asked.

Mr. Hocking stood there for a full minute, thinking, but he was licked and he knew it. Finally he threw up both hands and shook his head.

"Then it would seem," Justice Frazier said, looking at the photograph and speaking very slowly, "that Professor Pesman was murdered on June 11th, sometime between a quarter to one and a quarter to two by person or persons unknown, that the murder took place at point X, and that the body was moved to point Y where the defendant found it at eleven minutes after two. What can you offer to refute that conclusion?"

Mr. Hocking didn't say anything.

Justice Frazier rapped twice on the table. "I do not find probable cause to believe that the defendant committed the crime. I hereby dismiss the charges against the defendant, and release the defendant from custody."

Things were pretty confused tor the next few minutes. Mr. Hocking cornered Old Man Temple, and started an argument, only Mr. Hocking did the arguing and Mr. Temple mostly stood there grinning. A lot of people gathered around Mark Vaughan to congratulate him, Willie among them, and quite a few people went up to talk with Ted Frazier.

Then Mr. Boyd and Mrs. Glover came pushing their way through to the end of the room and Ted Frazier asked them what he could do for them.

"If you have the time," Mr. Boyd said, "we'd like to be married."

CHAPTER XIV

On Tuesday morning Grandfather received a statement from Strobel, Ross, Beal and Larkins for the ten shares of stock he'd ordered. I asked him if he'd changed his mind about buying them, and he said it was a little late to be changing his mind when the stock was already bought. He wrote out a check, and sent me over to the post office to mail it. I came back by way of the alley, and when I walked around the house Willie and Mark Vaughan were there, getting out of Vaughan's car.

It was the first time I'd ever seen Willie in a dress. With her short hair her face still looked a little like a boy's, but the rest of her certainly didn't. She wasn't wearing those silly glasses, or walking in the funny way that Willie had walked, and I thought that once her hair grew out she'd be a real pretty girl.

"Hi, Johnny," she said. "Is your grandfather home?"

I told them he was home, but I wouldn't guarantee how hospitable he would be. I didn't know how he might be taking spending all that money for stock. Sometimes when Grandfather reaches for his checkbook there's a terrible backlash.

There wasn't any this time. He met us at the front door, and shook hands with Mr. Vaughan and Willie, and invited them in just as if he hadn't spent any money for weeks.

We all sat down in the living room, and before our chairs had even started to get warm Mr. Vaughan said, "Mr. Rastin, who killed Professor Pesman?"

"That's no way to start a conversation," Grandfather said. "You're supposed to lead off with something simple, such as how to pay off the national debt, and move up to your difficult questions gradually. When you began with a question like that you don't leave yourself anywhere to go."

"That's what I was afraid of," Mr. Vaughan said.

Willie spoke very seriously. "You see, the case against Mark has been dismissed, but we have a feeling that the sheriff still suspects him. And as soon as the sheriff stops suspecting him he's going to start suspecting me, because I haven't a whisper of an alibi for the time the professor was murdered, and the sheriff will think my motive was almost as good as Mark's. We'll be surrounded by suspicion until the murder is solved. And besides—"

"Regardless of what other people thought of the professor," Mr. Vaughan said, "he was very generous to both of us. I can't think badly of a man who regarded my father highly enough to leave a fortune to him, and Willie feels grateful for more important things than the fifty thousand dollars he left to her. We want the murderer caught."

"The only person likely to disagree with you is the murderer," Grandfather said.

"I have a personal grudge against that murderer," Mr. Vaughan said. "I have a feeling that if I'd been convicted he'd have let me go to the electric chair without so much as a twitch of conscience."

"There isn't any death penalty in Michigan," Grandfather said, "but for a young man like you life in prison can seem like an awfully long time."

"We want to hire you to find the murderer," Willie said. "We don't think the sheriff will ever accomplish anything by himself, and with Mark a stranger here, and myself practically one we feel absolutely helpless to do anything about it. You can hire the detectives, or do whatever you think necessary, and we'll pay the bills."

Grandfather shook his head. "I couldn't accept a proposition like that."

"Why not?" Vaughan said. "I know you've already had some expenses. You went to Ohio, and found the information that got me arrested."

"You're going to pay me for that?" Grandfather asked.

"Why not? I know you didn't mean it personally, and in the long run it may help."

"Charlie Pesman was a friend of mine. I don't need to be paid to catch his murderer. If I can do it, I will."

"But you can't refuse to let us furnish you with the money you need to do the job," Vaughan said.

"Listen, you two," Grandfather said. "Both of you have suddenly gotten rich, and right away you think money is the answer to everything. It Isn't. If I thought money would catch the Professor's murderer I'd say write me a blank check and I'll go after him. I'm pretty sure money won't help a bit, so I don't want any. I wouldn't know what to do with it if you gave it to me. The only thing that will catch this murderer is brains, and if I have them, I'll get him. If I don't have them, money won't buy them for me."

"Suppose we were to offer a reward," Vaughan said. "Certainly you won't refuse a reward."

"That's a fine idea," Willie said.

"We'll offer ten thousand dollars," Vaughan said, "for—how do they say it? Information leading to the arrest and conviction, or something like that."

"We'll each put up five thousand," Willie said.

Vaughan turned and looked at her. "Don't be silly. I'm getting four hundred thousand, and you're only getting fifty thousand. I'll put up all of it."

"You will not," Willie said. "He was my stepfather, and you never even knew him. You can put up anything you like, but *I'm* offering five thousand."

"Whoa, there!" Grandfather said. "I won't have squabbling over money in my house."

Willie turned away from Mr. Vaughan long enough to notice me, and she said, "Johnny, it isn't polite to stare at a lady that way."

"I'm sorry," I said, "but you're the only man I ever knew that turned out to be a woman, and I was wondering if maybe you'd change back again."

Mr. Vaughan laughed. "She will not. You certainly must have an odd bunch of people in these parts. How Willie could spend two solid summers here without anyone so much as suspecting she was a girl is more than I'll ever understand. I knew it as soon as I laid eyes on her."

"You did not," Willie said. "You didn't know until Mr. Temple introduced me as the professor's stepdaughter, and then you had the colossal nerve to make an idiotic remark about me being a tomboy."

"That was before I'd seen you in a dress," Vaughan said. "You'll have to admit that there wasn't anything particularly glamorous about that baggy shirt and those patched pants you were wearing."

"The money's already gone to your head," Willie said. "You're a rich playboy looking for glamour. There are few feminine qualities that men of character—"

"That isn't what I meant at all. I didn't say you weren't glamorous, I just said that in that shirt—"

"Whoa, there!" Grandfather said. "I won't have glamour discussed in this house either. I thought you two wanted to catch a murderer."

"Have you any idea at all as to who did it?" Willie said.

"I have a little bit of an idea who did it," Grandfather said. "And I think I know how it was done. But I've put miles on my rocking chair with an arm in a sling—and I just can't figure out why it was done. When it comes to bringing a murderer to justice the 'Why' may be just as important as the 'Who' and the 'How,' and this particular 'Why' looks to me to be awfully complicated. It could be that we will have to hire an expert or two to help us out."

"Let me know when," Vaughan said, "and I'll make the necessary financial arrangements."

"You will not," Willie said. "We agreed that we'd go together—"

"Never mind," Grandfather said. "There's no point in arguing about who's going to pay the experts, when we don't even know what kind of experts we need. What are you going to do with the Courthouse?"

"I haven't decided yet," Vaughan said. "Junior wants to consult with me today about hiring a caretaker, and that's all I'm going to worry about for the present. When I have time I'll have to go over the situation and see what the upkeep will amount to. I'm sure the farmland is valuable, but it probably would be difficult to get a fair price for the house."

"I tried to buy it," Willie said. "He won't sell it to me. He even got me fired as caretaker."

"I offered to pay your salary through the summer," Vaughan said. "You know a girl has no business living there by herself."

"No one cared before," Willie said.

"Mr. Rastin," Vaughan said, "is there any civilized way to win an argument with a woman?"

"I don't know," Grandfather said. "I've never tried."

"I'm not going to let Willie sink all of her money into a white elephant, no matter how much sentimental attachment she may have for it."

"I spent the happiest moments of my life there," Willie said. "To him, that's a sentimental attachment. To a man, a house is something to sell. To a woman, it's a place to live. I want to live in the Courthouse, and teach at Wiston College. That's my destiny—to be an old maid college teacher. His is to write scandalous best-selling historical novels about the wives of the presidents."

"Did anyone ever tell you that you talk too much?" Vaughan asked.

Willie laughed. "No one around here ever did."

"Willie," Grandfather said, "no one bothered to question you about what happened the day the professor was killed because we all thought you couldn't talk. Supposing you answer a few questions now."

"I've asked myself all kinds of questions," Willie said. "The answers don't help any. All I have to contribute is my tale of watching Mark flounder around the maze."

"You'll have to admit I did pretty well," Vaughan said. "Boyd told me few people ever got as far as I did."

"He was just being polite. I've seen Mr. Jones's dog do a better job blindfolded."

"That doesn't prove anything. Dogs see with their noses."

"What is it that you see with?"

Vaughan got to his feet wearily. "As you can see, she did a smart thing pretending to be dumb."

"The word is 'mute'," Willie said.

"Call it anything you like. If she hadn't pretended she couldn't talk, the professor would never have left her a penny. You'll tell us, won't you, if there's anything we can do? And if money can help—"

"I'll let you know," Grandfather said.

We all shook hands, and then they went back to the car, Vaughan saying along the way, "The reward is a good idea, but since I inherited most of the money I should put up most of it. How about nine thousand and one thousand?"

"That's ridiculous," Willie said. "Anyway, your four hundred thousand to my fifty thousand is only eight to one."

They drove away.

"They'll be married inside a month," Grandfather said.

"What makes you think that?" I asked. "It looked to me as if they were mad at each other all the time, the way they argued."

"If two people can disagree that much and still stand the sight of each other, they have to be in love," Grandfather said. "When Sheriff Pilkins comes, send him up. What are you grinning about?"

"I was thinking about you and Sheriff Pilkins. You argue all the time, but you still—"

"Horse feathers!" Grandfather said, and went upstairs.

I expected Sheriff Pilkins to be in a glum mood, and I wasn't disappointed. For the second time in this one murder case he'd had a bright idea blow up right under his nose, and I got the impression that he wasn't about to let it happen again. For all of his wild notions I've never heard anyone say the sheriff wasn't an honest man, and I think he'd rather arrest nobody at all than the wrong person. The way he looked that day, he'd just about made up his mind it had to be nobody at all.

I took him up to Grandfather's bedroom, and got a chair for him and for a long time neither he nor Grandfather said anything. "You told me," the sheriff said finally, "that you knew who the murderer is."

"I said I thought I knew," Grandfather said.

"Naturally I wouldn't expect you to come right out and tell a sheriff a little thing like the identity of a murderer."

"What would you do if I did?" Grandfather asked.

"I'd arrest him."

"That's your trouble. You're real good at arresting people, but you're no good at all at proving you had some reason for arresting them. What's the point in arresting the murderer if you can't prove he is the murderer?"

"I can't even try to prove it if I don't know who it is."

"It's better that way," Grandfather said. "It keeps you out of trouble."

The sheriff's complexion shifted from neutral to pink. "You must have had something in mind, or you wouldn't have asked me to come over here."

"I have two things in mind," Grandfather said. "It's occurred to me that we really don't know very much about what the professor did with his maze. He staged a lot of experiments with a lot of different people, and if we knew who all those people were we might have a lot of names to add to our list of suspects."

"I suppose so," the sheriff said. "How do we find out who they were?"

"Have you looked in the professor's filing cabinets? He has a record there of every experiment he ever conducted—with the name of the person he conducted it on."

"I know," the sheriff said. "I heard Willie yesterday, but I didn't think much about it. I'll get to work on it right away."

"It isn't quite that simple. There are lots of drawers there, and they're packed from end to end. It may take you a week. And one thing more—it wouldn't do for the murderer to know you're doing this."

"I don't see what difference it makes," the sheriff said. "But you said you had two things on your mind."

"Yes. I'd like to set a trap for the murderer."

"I'm all in favor of anything that will get me close to the guy. Just tell me where you want the trap, and I'll make the arrangements."

"It isn't simple, either," Grandfather said. "A trap won't work worth a darn if we don't bait it, and so far I haven't been able to think of anything I could use for bait."

The sheriff had to think that one over, and while he thought, Grandfather rocked and watched him. Though the sheriff has been squabbling with Grandfather for more years than I am old, he has never quite understood him, but he has learned that whenever Grandfather starts spreading bait around he has to be careful not to swallow some himself.

"I think I get it," he said. "These records of the professor could be the bait."

"It's a possibility," Grandfather said.

"And that's why you don't want anyone to know I'm working on them." Grandfather nodded.

"What do you want me to do?"

"Get those records out of the Courthouse and into a safe place. But it'll have to be done after dark, and with a minimum fuss."

"Do Vaughan and Willie know about this? And Junior Temple?"

"Not yet," Grandfather said. "But there won't be any trouble there. Vaughan wants the murderer caught, and so does Willie. They'll even help you go over the records, if you ask them. As for Temple—you don't have to tell him, do you? The records are evidence, and as he'd say, he has no responsibility."

"I'll get the records tonight," the sheriff said. "There's a room in the basement of the County Building that we can use. It'll be a safe place to keep them, and we can work on them right there. I don't quite understand what it is we're supposed to do with the records, though."

"I'd start by making a list of all the people the professor experimented with."

"Who, and how many times," the sheriff suggested.

"Yes. The number of times would be important."

"I'll see Vaughan right away, and make the arrangements. And when you're ready to bring your trap into it, you let me know. Do you want to help out with the records?"

"I couldn't sit still long enough to do a job like that, but there are a couple of things about those records I'd like to check into. You give me a call when you have them moved, and Johnny will bring me over."

"Right."

"What will you do—put them in boxes?"

"We could take the cabinets, but I suppose it'd be a job getting them down from the top floor. I can get some cardboard boxes that are the same size as the file drawers, and they'll be a lot easier to carry."

"Do it that way," Grandfather said. "But be sure to mark them with the labels the professor has on the filing cabinets. You may have a mess on your hands if you mix them up."

"We'll be careful," the sheriff said.

He was in such a hurry to get away and start making arrangements that I didn't get to go to the door with him. He was out of the house before I started down the stairway. I went back and told Grandfather he shouldn't have done that.

Grandfather was rocking slowly with a satisfied look on his face, and he chuckled, and asked me what I meant.

"In school we have a word for it," I said. "It's called 'busywork.' It's work the teachers give us so we'll stay busy and out of trouble."

"That's a good word," Grandfather said. "'Busywork.' Pilkins is in a desperate mood, and Vaughan and Willie are going to be clamoring for action and swooping around like a pair of drunk bats at high noon, and turning the three of them loose to solve this murder would be like giving a watch repair job to a man with a sledge hammer. Those records will keep their minds off other things for at least a couple of days, and I hope that's all the time I need."

"The sheriff won't appreciate your pulling his leg like this," I said.

"Maybe I'm not. This idea of mine may turn out to be as idiotic as those Pilkins has had, and if it does those files may come in useful. Anything will come in useful. Do we have a magnifying glass in the house?"

"I have one in my stamp collection," I said. "What are you going to do now—play Sherlock Holmes? If it's fingerprints you're after, you ought to let the sheriff handle it. He can get the right equipment."

"If Pilkins ever starts going over the Courthouse for fingerprints, he'll be arresting *me* for murder. There are plenty of mine there."

CHAPTER XV

Tuesday afternoon Grandfather and I went secretly to the Courthouse, so Grandfather could have a last crack at the professor's records before the sheriff took over. We didn't have anyone's permission to do this, but the new caretaker, who was Pete Kruger, felt so deeply indebted to Grandfather that he would have allowed us to steal anything in the place as long as it wasn't an animal.

This was not merely because Pete thought Grandfather had saved him from the sheriff. After the preliminary hearing Grandfather persuaded Mr. Vaughan to let Pete have the white mouse called Herman for his very own, and also a mate for Herman, if there was one of the right sex among the other laboratory animals. These gifts were not legal, because the professor's property would not officially belong to Mr. Vaughan for months, or maybe even years if you wanted to believe Junior Temple but Mr. Vaughan decided that he might as well make an illegal dispensation of such things as white mice before they succumbed to senility while waiting for Junior Temple to make something happen.

Pete thanked him with tears in his eyes, and promised Mr. Vaughan two of the first litter of Herman's babies, only Mr. Vaughan was not quite as enthused about this offer as Pete seemed to think he should be.

So Pete turned the Courthouse over to us, all except the animal cages, and when Grandfather asked him not to tell anyone we'd been there he said he'd already forgotten about it.

I don't know very much about what Grandfather did that afternoon, because he put me to work on the professor's library, which was scattered not only all around the laboratory, but all over the house. He wanted me to leaf through the books looking for important papers that might have been tucked away there, such as a confession signed by the murderer, or maybe a secret will. I leafed through one book, and then I took careful note of the 9,999 that were left, and worked out a system by which I held the book so the pages hung loose, and shook it. I didn't find any important papers, but I did find a lot of cigarette papers that someone in the house was in the habit of using for bookmarks.

While I was doing this Grandfather worked on the filing cabinets, and once I saw him actually using my magnifying glass for about four minutes. When we'd finished he carried away a big envelope full of papers, which he took back to Borgville to the Borgville Savings Bank for Mr. Hansen, the bank president, to lock in the safe. He had a private conference with Mr. Hansen about those papers, and when he came out I asked him if Mr. Hansen was the expert he was hiring.

"Hansen isn't an expert in anything," Grandfather said. "He's only a bank president. But at least he hasn't any personal connections with this business, and he is reliable and can keep his mouth shut."

Grandfather went home to his rocking chair, and I spent the rest of the afternoon trying to get Mom's permission to ask Mr. Vaughan for an illegal dispensation of my favorite guinea pig.

The sheriff telephoned about ten o'clock that night to say that he'd emptied the filing cabinets and had all the stuff at the County Building. Grandfather said fine, but he'd decided not to come to Wiston that night. The sheriff could carry on, and he'd look in on him in the morning. Then Grandfather went right to bed and slept soundly. At least, I think he slept soundly, because his snoring woke me up three times during the night.

Wednesday morning I took him to Wiston, and first he looked after a few personal matters, such as telling the real estate agent he'd decided not to sell his house, and inspecting the job of painting Bob Meyers had done, and showing the house to some prospective tenants. After that we stopped at the County Building, and Grandfather spent a half hour looking over shoulders while two deputies and Willie and Mr. Vaughan worked on the records and took notes.

Mr. Vaughan was still chuckling over Pete Kruger's reaction when he told him he could have Herman. "I never thought I'd see a grown man cry real tears over a mouse," he said. "It makes me wonder if the great events of history happened for the reasons they did. Perhaps behind every political upheaval stands a white mouse. I'm going to look into it."

"Why don't you start now," Willie said, "and quit distracting us with gossip?"

"You think I didn't hear you telling the deputies those stories Boyd told you when he thought you were a man?"

The deputies giggled and looked embarrassed. Grandfather said he had grave doubts that any of them would get any work done unless the sheriff put in partitions, and he would speak to him about it. We did go over to the sheriff's office, but the sheriff wasn't in, and Grandfather told the deputy on duty there that it wasn't important anyway, and he'd telephone the sheriff later.

From there we went up to the County Attorney's office, where everyone was still in mourning over Mark Vaughan's preliminary hearing. "When you people get through crying over spilled milk," Grandfather said, "I'd suggest that you check the bank accounts of Evan Boyd and Ruth Glover

Boyd. Boyd said he saved ten thousand dollars in ten years, and that's quite an accomplishment for a man who makes a hundred and fifty a month and likes to drink."

"It is, at that," Mr. Hocking said, reaching for a memo pad. "We're also checking into the background of Miss Wilhelmina Davis. We have only her word for it that she's the professor's stepdaughter. As a matter of fact, we have only her word for it she's a she."

"Have you seen her since the hearing?" Grandfather said.

"No, I haven't."

"She's downstairs doing some work for Pilkins. I'd suggest that you go down and have a look."

The next stop was the Temple law offices, where Grandfather had a long conversation with Old Man Temple on the subject of Lyle Jones's records. Mr. Temple agreed to have someone who knew something about farming look the records over, but he didn't seem very enthusiastic about the job.

"Jones is honest," he said, "and he's a good farmer."

"A murderer," Grandfather said, "often has many excellent qualities. I've even heard tell of some who loved their mothers."

"I'll see that it's taken care of," Mr. Temple said.

"And if you want us for anything," Grandfather said, "I'll be at home."

On the way back to Borgville I asked him if he had his trap baited yet.

"I have maybe five different kinds of traps," he said, "and they're all baited. I'm going to set them one at a time, the most likely one first."

I wanted to know what would happen if the murderer snatched the bait from a trap before he got it set, and he told me there were limits beyond which one should not attempt to stretch a figure of speech.

"Then why do you need so many traps?" I asked.

"Johnny," he said, "some years ago there was a poultry farmer north of Borgville who was losing his chickens. They kept disappearing, and no amount of work on his henhouses seemed to make them safe. He knew about an old coon that had been around there for years, and he decided the coon was getting his chickens. He set all the traps he could get a hold of, and finally he got that coon. His chickens kept right on disappearing. Then he thought maybe the neighbor's dog was responsible. One afternoon he cornered the dog on his property, and shot it, making a lifelong enemy out of his neighbor. The chickens still disappeared. For a couple of weeks he sat up nights trying to catch someone stealing them. He didn't and they kept disappearing."

"What was taking them," I asked.

"His wife. She was dressing them and selling them, and when she got enough money saved up she ran away and got a divorce."

Sheriff Pilkins telephoned right after lunch and Grandfather told him to call back after six. After that it was a dull afternoon, except when Mr. Hansen telephoned, and Grandfather listened, nodding his head.

The clock had just started to strike six when Sheriff Pilkins called back. "Everything is ready," Grandfather told him. "Now listen. This is what I want you to do."

Grandfather gave him a long list of instructions, and the sheriff listened. If he argued at all it didn't come through at our end, because Grandfather didn't even pause until he'd finished.

"Have you got all that?" Grandfather asked. "Or shall I go over it again?"

The sheriff had all of it.

"Send a car for us," Grandfather said, and hung up.

The sheriff sent a car for us, and a little after dark it deposited us at the Courthouse and drove away. I thought this was a silly waste of transportation, since someone would also have to take us home. "We could have left our car at the Jones farm," I said. "No one would see it there."

"Who is 'no one'?" Grandfather asked.

The sheriff, some deputies, and also a couple of State Police troopers, were sitting in the living room with the lights off, listening to Vaughan and Willie argue about whether it would be better to replaster the ceiling, or just cover the old plaster with wall paper. Vaughan favored the wall paper, because, he said, no one but a moron would sink any more money into that house than was absolutely necessary. Willie thanked him, and said she had some observations on *his* intelligence that she'd like to pass along, but she'd wait until there were a few more people present to hear them.

"It's about time you got here," the sheriff said to Grandfather. "Those two are beginning to get on my nerves."

"All it takes to solve a problem like that is organization," Grandfather said. "Willie!"

"Yes, *sir*!" Willie said.

"Your post is up in the laboratory. Beat it."

"Aye, aye, sir," Willie said, and headed for the stairway.

"Vaughan, I have a job for you in the basement. Go ahead, and I'll be down in a minute to show you what to do."

"Right," Vaughan said, and went to the basement.

"Any questions?" Grandfather asked the sheriff.

"If I'd told them to do that, they'd have sent me to the basement and gone on arguing."

Grandfather got everyone posted without trouble, though I think he would have had some odd looks from the deputies if we'd been able to see them. He had each man armed with a fire extinguisher, and even the sheriff seemed to think that these were odd weapons for capturing a murderer.

"One would be enough," he said. "We won't give him time to light more than a cigarette."

"I never underestimate a crook," Grandfather said.

The sheriff, though he didn't know exactly what Grandfather was up to, was feeling agreeable about all the arrangements except one. "Why let him get all the way up to the top floor?" He asked. "Why not grab him when he comes through the door?"

"Because," Grandfather said, "I want to establish that he came here for a purpose, and not just a social call. Johnny, I want you up with Willie."

"Aye, aye, sir," I said, and climbed the stairs.

Willie had put a hamster in the maze. She said it was a nocturnal animal, and she thought it would do better at night, but the professor had never let her try it, and she hadn't figured out a way to tell him what she meant without talking. I told her that the events of the past couple of weeks had cooled me on the subject of mazes for good, so she put the hamster back in its cage and asked me what I thought of Mark Vaughan.

This sort of question always embarrasses me. I really don't think anything special of anyone—I just sort of accept people the way they are. "I guess he's good looking," I said.

She took a deep breath, and said, "He certainly is."

"I liked you better when you were a boy," I said.

"You're too young to realize what a terrible insult that is," she said. "But never mind. You'll grow up, and fall in love yourself one day."

"Are you in love with Mr. Vaughan?" I asked.

"I certainly am," she said. "I fell for him the first time I saw him—when I was watching him in the maze."

"From the way you argue with him all the time, I'd have thought you didn't like him very much."

"That's so he won't know I'm chasing him," she said. "Boys don't like girls to chase them."

"They sure don't," I said.

"But if girls didn't chase boys, it might never occur to the boys to chase the girls, and life would be in a terrible mess."

I had to think that one over. "You mean if a girl acts mean to you she's doing it so you won't know she's chasing you, and she doesn't want you to know she's chasing you so you'll chase her?"

"Right."

"I wonder if that's why Sue Busby let the air out of my tires at the Junior Prom."

"Probably," she said. "Did you start chasing her?"

"I sure did," I said. "I was mad enough to break her neck, but I couldn't catch her because she had too much of a head start."

"That isn't exactly what I meant," Willie said. "But never mind. One of these days you'll understand. Anyway, I'm going to marry Mark Vaughan, but not until I've made him do some fancy chasing."

"Does he know that?"

"Certainly not! And don't you dare tell him."

"He wouldn't believe me if I did."

"Of course he would," she said. "A man as good-looking as he is has had so many girls fall for him that he comes to expect it. That's why I want him to think I don't like him."

"You've taught me one thing, anyway," I said.

"What's that?"

"I'm going to keep a long way away from any girl who's been studying psychology."

Grandfather came in and handed each one of us a camera. He said they were part of an idea he had, and though he doubted the idea would work there wasn't any harm in trying. "They've been set by an expert," he said. "All you have to do is aim and let fly. I'll nudge Willie when I want her to shoot and you wait about three seconds, Johnny and let yours go. If we time it right the first one will catch him with his hand in a filing cabinet. Naturally when the flash bulb goes off he'll jump and turn around, and the second one should get him facing the camera."

"When is all this due to happen?" I asked.

"That's a silly question," Grandfather said, "and you know it."

Willie went and sat down on the floor in the corner. She said she'd gotten used to sitting on the floor while she was pretending to be a man, and now she liked it. When she had her own house she was going to keep one corner bare in every room so she could sit there when she felt like it. I suggested that she keep two corners bare, so she could offer one to a guest, and Grandfather said if the two of us didn't keep quiet he'd send one of us down to the basement, and that one wouldn't be Willie.

There were only two chairs in the laboratory. Grandfather took one of them, and because the other one was the professor's desk chair Grandfather said it had to stay by his desk, so the place would look natural. There were things scattered around that I might have sat on if there'd been any light for me to see whether they'd break or not, but Grandfather wouldn't let me use my flashlight. I ended up in the corner opposite Willie, and it was then that I decided that I didn't want to be a detective. I don't mind a sitting-down job, but I think someone should furnish a chair.

The sheriff came up around midnight, and said everyone was in position, and things were perfectly quiet outside, and where was the murderer? Grandfather told him the murderer was home in bed, for all he knew, and the sheriff hadn't needed to come all the way up there just to ask a foolish question because there were already two people present who had some talent for that. Willie said if she had to be insulted she'd go down to the basement and listen to Mr. Vaughan's insults, and I said if the murderer was home in bed he had more sense that we did, and after the sheriff had jawed at Grandfather a little he went back downstairs feeling better.

The floor wasn't getting any softer, and I asked Grandfather twice if I could go down and get a chair. Both times he said the murderer would probably come and find me stuck in the narrow stairway that connected the laboratory with the second floor. Finally, after squirming around for what seemed to be an hour looking for a soft board, I fell asleep.

The next thing I knew Willie was shaking me awake, saying it was almost daylight, and everyone was going home.

Surprisingly enough, the sheriff had very little to say to Grandfather. Their argument didn't last more than ten minutes, and the sheriff wound it up by saying, for the fifth time, "You told me you had the trap baited."

"I did have it baited," Grandfather said.

"Where's the murderer, then?"

"Maybe he didn't smell the bait. Or maybe he got scared. Say—I wonder. Vaughan!"

"What is it?" Mr. Vaughan asked.

"How many people know Pete Kruger was hired as caretaker?"

"I haven't any idea. The Temples, of course, and we didn't make any effort to keep it a secret."

"Maybe that's it. Where's Pete?"

A deputy went to find him, and he came in with Herman in his hand. "Pete," Grandfather said, "have you any relatives you'd like to visit?"

"I got a cousin in Wiston," Pete said.

"I mean out of town."

"I got a sister in Chicago, but I ain't seen her since—since—"

"You're going to see her," Grandfather said. "You just had word that she's sick and not expected to live."

"Gosh, that's too bad," Pete said. "She's got seven kids, and her health never was very good."

"Tell everyone we'll try again tonight," Grandfather told the sheriff. "And Pete, you come in here. You too, Vaughan. This will take some working out."

The sheriff was feeling too bewildered to object. He told his deputies more of the same that night, and I went into the dining room and found a chair with a nice padded seat and carried it up to the laboratory.

When I came down Grandfather was still trying to convince Pete that he should go to Chicago. He agreed, finally—after Vaughan had promised to pay for his bus ticket and keep his salary going, and after Grandfather convinced him that Herman could ride along on the bus, providing that Pete kept him in his pocket all the way. Grandfather sent the sheriff to telephone for a bus schedule, and then he had more instructions for Mr. Vaughan, and finally everything was arranged.

"He'd better smell the bait this time," the sheriff said.

"I'll wave it under his nose," Grandfather promised.

A deputy drove us home, and we ate a good breakfast and went right to bed.

I slept until after noon, and when I went downstairs Grandfather had already eaten. I asked him if he'd waved the bait, and he said he had, and that Mr. Vaughan had put Pete on the ten-thirty bus, and if all concerned could keep their mouths shut we had a reasonable chance of getting the murderer.

"Supposing we don't?" I said.

"Then I'll have to think of something else."

"Whatever it is, be sure to include a chair for me."

That night Grandfather made one change in the arrangements. It suddenly occurred to him that the murderer was the same one who'd used us for target practice in the maze, and he decided he wanted an armed man up in the laboratory with us. He told one of the deputies to wait up there with his fire extinguisher, and when I went up darned if the guy wasn't using my chair. I made him get one for himself.

We settled down for another long wait, and for maybe an hour no one said anything. Then Willie started to recite, "'Twas the night before Christmas, and all through the house—" which wasn't exactly true, because there were a lot of things stirring in those laboratory cages. Anyway Grandfather hushed Willie before she even got to the clatter on the lawn.

Nothing else happened for a long time, and I tilted back in my chair and almost dozed off. I think everyone else was in approximately the same mental condition, and that's how it happened that the murderer walked right in on us before we even knew he was on his way.

There'd been one little weakness in Grandfather's plan, and he admitted it himself afterwards, though not while Sheriff Pilkins was there to hear him. The Courthouse was a big place, and when the murderer started to break in there wasn't any way the ones hiding downstairs could let the ones hiding upstairs know what was going on.

The murderer did a real professional job of housebreaking, putting tape on one of the little windows in the rear door so he could break the glass without making a noise, and reach in and turn the night lock. The sheriff said afterwards that he'd gone to a lot of trouble for nothing, because if the house had been empty the way he thought it was he could have heaved a brick through the living room window, but I think he was exaggerating. Anyway, the only one who knew the murderer was coming was Mr. Vaughan, who was watching from a basement window by the door.

Up in the laboratory we didn't hear anything at all. If the murderer had flashed a light around the room before he started for the filing cabinets, he'd have caught four sitting ducks with their bare faces hanging out, and what followed might not have been pleasant because he did have a loaded revolver in his pocket. But having gotten that far he figured he was in free, and he headed for the filing cabinet nearest the professor's desk and jerked the drawer open.

The drawer was empty, of course, and he slammed it shut and opened another one, and then a third one, and then he moved over to the next cabinet. By that time he was acting panicky, and he didn't hear us start to move around.

Willie tiptoed up to the maze, where she was supposed to stand for her picture. She couldn't get a signal from Grandfather, because Grandfather was over by the wall and hadn't moved. She snapped her picture at what she figured to be the right time—and caught the murderer with a hand in a drawer, it turned out—and by then I'd eased my chair back to the floor and was on my way to join her. I wasn't quite in position, but I counted three and let fly, and the murderer had spun around just as Grandfather had predicted. He had a cloth over his face, with holes cut for his eyes, and he looked like the bad man out of a horse opera.

As I took my picture Grandfather jumped for the light switch, and the deputy sheriff came up from his chair with the fire extinguisher in one hand and his gun in the other.

I didn't notice the gallon can of gasoline until the murderer dove for it. He had it tipped over before any of us could move, and his cigarette lighter out, and the next thing there was a blast of flame that filled the whole end of the room. The deputy dropped his revolver and went to work with his fire extinguisher, and the other five deputies came charging in with their fire extinguishers and in a matter of seconds they had the fire out and the murderer pretty well soaked. He hadn't even been hurt except for his clothes and hair being singed. The sheriff, galloping up on the heels of the last deputy with Mr. Vaughan and the two State Police troopers following him, stood in the light rubbing his eyes, and Grandfather said, "All right—you've got him. Take him away."

The sheriff rubbed his eyes again. "Who is he?"

"Jerry Krohl," Grandfather said. "Who else?"

CHAPTER XVI

Two deputies took Krohl's gun, and ripped his mask off, and pinned him up against the wall, and if you think the sheriff was hopping for joy you're wrong.

First he wanted to argue. "It can't be Krohl," he said.

"Can't it?" Grandfather said.

"Krohl has never been in the maze. I checked that myself last week, and I know his name isn't on any of those records the professor kept. Any you said yourself it had to be someone who knew the maze."

"Did I?" Grandfather said.

"You did," the sheriff said, getting madder as he talked. "I suppose you knew all along it was Krohl, and you just said that to head me in the wrong direction so you could keep me up all night watching you play games."

Grandfather turned to the deputies, and pointed to the stairway. "Take him away."

The deputies looked at the sheriff. The sheriff glared at Grandfather.

"Take him away," Grandfather said again. "It isn't good to have a criminal know that the officer that caught him is a dunce."

"Now just a minute," the sheriff said. "I'm not arresting him on your say-so. You'll have to prove to me that he did it. I don't want to charge another man with murder, and then—"

"Charge him with attempted arson, then!" Grandfather said. "And get him out of here!"

The deputies very timidly led Krohl away.

"Now then," Grandfather said. "If you want to know *why* Krohl did it, that's complicated, and it's too late to get started on it now. I aim to get some sleep tonight. If you want to know *how* he did it, I can show you that in about fifteen minutes."

"You'd better," the sheriff said.

"Where's Willie?" Grandfather asked.

She was already down in the kitchen, arguing about something with Vaughan. Grandfather pried them apart, and we all went outside by the maze.

"We'll need a couple of flashlights," Grandfather said.

Six were handed to him, from all directions.

"Now, then," he said. "This is how I figured it happened. Krohl had never been in the maze and the professor was always after him to give it a try. The longer Krohl held out, the more eager the professor got. If there'd been another broker in town the professor might have threatened to take his business elsewhere, but there wasn't, and Krohl was doing a good job for him, so he got away with it.

"Then he decided to kill the professor."

"Why?" Sheriff Pilkins asked.

Grandfather ignored him. "He was here to see the professor that day, and he left not long after twelve thirty. Just before he left he suggested that he might be willing to give the maze a try, but on a confidential basis. Maybe he said he was afraid he wouldn't do well, and he didn't want the others giving him the horse laugh. The professor was delighted to accept on any basis, so they made their arrangements. Krohl would drive around by the road and leave his car there, and the professor would go through the maze and meet him, and no one in the house would see what was going on because the professor would say he was doing a special experiment and keep everyone out of the laboratory."

"There wasn't any car parked on the road," the Sheriff said. "I checked. No one saw a car before Vaughan showed up."

"Do you want to tell this yourself?" Grandfather asked.

"Go on," the sheriff muttered.

"Krohl had been coming here long enough to know the setup perfectly, and maybe at the last minute he said, "No, I'd better not do it. Someone would hear the bell ring.' Maybe he expected the professor to turn the bell off, or some such thing. But the professor told him the electric eye gadget that makes the bell ring is three feet off the ground, and all he had to do was crawl under it. Or maybe Krohl already knew that."

"It used to be lower," Willie said, "but one day a couple of dogs kept running in and out, and the professor had it raised."

"So everything was arranged. Krohl left and the professor announced that he was doing a special experiment. Instead of going up to the laboratory, as everyone thought, he went out through the maze to meet Krohl. Meantime, Krohl drove around and parked his car out of sight in Jones's wood lot. There's a short drive in there that young people have maybe been using for personal activities, and you may find Krohl's tire marks there. He used it again when he caught Johnny and me in the maze. He picked a moment when there was no traffic on the highway, and ran down to the maze, and got in without ringing the bell."

"He took a chance on being seen," the sheriff said.

"I doubt if it's possible to engineer a murder without taking chances," Grandfather said. "The professor had decided to give him the business, and he took him as far into the maze as he ever took anyone. That suited Krohl.

They got to where they were going, and synchronized watches so the professor would have time to get up to the laboratory before Krohl started trying to find his way out, or maybe Krohl didn't wait for that. He had the pipe in his briefcase, and he let the professor have it. He figured he had the best alibi in the world because no one would think he could have found his way out of the maze, but when he saw the fence post he tried to complicated matters further by making it look as if the professor had bumped his head accidently. Either way it was a pretty fair plan, and I'd guess that inside of twenty minutes after he slugged the professor he was on his way back to town. Naturally he avoided ringing the bell on the way out, and he made sure the road was clear before he ran back to the woodlot."

"He took a chance," the sheriff said.

"But not much of a chance. It's only a little over a hundred yards from the maze entrance to the woodlot. A sprinter can do that in ten seconds, and it wouldn't take an active man like Krohl any more than twenty. If a car had come along it wouldn't have gotten close enough for the driver to see who he was."

"You still haven't explained how he got out of the maze."

"I won't explain. I'll show you. Willie, will you place me in the maze?"

"I'd be delighted," Willie said.

The sheriff still wasn't sure he liked what was going on. "Just a minute," he said. "The professor and Krohl went in from the other side."

"Drat it!" Grandfather said. "I'm not acting out the murder. I'm just showing how Krohl got out of the maze."

"All right," the sheriff said. "But Willie, be sure you take him at least as far as the professor took Krohl."

"Don't worry," Willie said. "I don't know what he's got up his sleeve, but it'll have to be good if he can find his way out from where I'll take him."

Grandfather said he would signal with his flashlight when he was ready to start back, and Willie said she'd wait and follow him, in case he got lost. The sheriff sent a deputy up to the laboratory to watch for Grandfather's signal, and the rest of us stood around waiting.

The deputy called down from an open window. "He's coming," and we all looked at our watches and started timing. It was just twelve minutes and twenty seconds later that Grandfather came strolling into view.

"And I will point out," he said, grinning into our gapping faces, "that I did it with a flashlight, and I didn't hurry. I could have made much better time in daylight."

Willie was right behind him, and she said disgustedly, "It's a fraud. While I was leading him in, he marked every turn by scraping a line in the gravel with his foot. It's been tried before, and we always thought it was a good joke, because on the way out we'd erase the marks, and even put in a few different marks if we felt like it, and that person would get the surprise of his life when he tried to follow them."

"It worked in Krohl's case," Grandfather said. "Maybe the professor saw what he was doing and planned to erase the marks on his way out, but it was a one-way trip for him. Krohl erased his own marks as he left, be he was in a hurry and didn't do a good job. I found most of them the other night."

"Then he figured you were onto something, and tried to shoot you," the sheriff said.

"That's the way I see it. I had Johnny telephone him for information about the stocks the professor had been buying, and then when I talked to him that afternoon he got the idea that I might be coming close. He must have followed us all evening, and when we went into the maze he decided it was time for action."

"You still haven't explained why," the sheriff said.

"Ask Krohl. And if he won't cooperate, Hansen, of the Borgville Bank may be able to tell you a few things of interest. As for me, if anyone rings my doorbell before noon tomorrow he gets a bucket of water on his head. Now take me home."

Mom was waiting up for us. "Is it over with?" she asked.

Grandfather told her it was.

"It's about time," she said.

I looked out of the front window at eleven thirty the next morning and the sheriff was sitting in his car waiting. At precisely noon he walked up onto our porch and rang the bell. "Is your grandfather up yet?" he asked.

Grandfather had been up for at least an hour, but I didn't think it would be diplomatic to tell him that. "Sit down and I'll see," I said. But he wouldn't sit down. He stood by the door and fussed with his hat, and when Grandfather came down and told him to have a chair he said he wouldn't stay but a minute, but he wanted Grandfather to know that Krohl had signed a confession, and the County Attorney thought that they would have an airtight case even without that.

"We have his briefcase," the sheriff said. "There are flecks of rust inside that will match those found in the wound, and also blood spots that came from the pipe after Krohl used it. What I'd like to know is, how did you get onto the fact that he was manipulating the professor's investment account?"

"Call it a hunch," Grandfather said.

"Hunch, nothing. And here's another thing. Hansen tells me you brought in the professor's brokerage account statements on Tuesday, and he called Strobel, Ross, Beal and Larkins in Detroit, at your request, and both of you knew for certain then that Krohl had been faking those statements. Why didn't you just have him arrested, instead of going through that fa-de-la at the Courthouse?"

"I didn't want him to wiggle out of it," Grandfather said. "I thought it was best to catch him in circumstances so incriminating that he'd figure he might as well confess."

"Well, he confessed. It happened just about the way you said, and I suppose I should thank you for your help."

"I suppose you should," Grandfather said.

"And I would have, if you hadn't kept me up all night for two nights in a row, and had me chasing all over the place, and put my whole department to sorting records that didn't mean anything. I don't appreciate that. So I won't thank you."

"I didn't think you would," Grandfather said.

"And anyway—" The sheriff's face had been gradually getting redder. "Aw, nuts to it," he said, and stomped out of the door.

"He's probably telling himself he'll never come back here again," I said.

"He won't," Grandfather said. "Until the next time."

Mr. Vaughan and Willie came while we were eating lunch. They told us to go ahead and finish, so we did, and when we went into the living room the first thing Willie had to show us was her new diamond engagement ring.

"I bought it on credit," Mr. Vaughan said. "Until the professor's estate is officially mine I'll be more broke than I ever was, because I now have a position to maintain. Fortunately my credit seems to be pretty good around here."

"Have you two set a date yet?" Grandfather asked.

"No," Vaughan said, "but it'll be right away. I've got a job teaching at Wiston College, and we're going to live in the Courthouse and have about a dozen children. If we're going to have a house that big we might as well use it."

"Nonsense," Willie said. "I'm going back to Holdon College in the fall. I'll graduate next spring, and then we'll get married. I want to be a June bride."

"You can be a June bride this year, Vaughan said.

"I cannot. It's already the twenty-eighth, and there isn't time. Anyway, by next spring I might change my mind. I may want to do graduate work in psychology."

"I don't think its right for you to make him go on chasing you after he's proposed," I said.

"Johnny," Willie said, "that was a very rude thing to say. I thought you were trustworthy."

"Trustworthy or not, Johnny has a point," Vaughan said. "Either we get married next month, or I'm selling the Courthouse and going back to Landsdorf College."

"If that's the way you feel about it, you can take your old ring back right now!"

"Thanks," Vaughan said. "I will." He took the ring, and put it in his pocket. "If your icy hand hasn't corroded it, I'll return it and get out of debt."

"Stop gloating," Willie said, "and tell them why we came."

"Oh. Yes. I have a certified check for ten thousand dollars. It's the reward money. I had to borrow this, too, but as I said, my credit is very good."

"*Our* credit is good," Willie said. "Part of it is from me."

"Yes. Well, Krohl has confessed, and I'm sure you're entitled to this, but we aren't going to give it to you until you tell us how you figured it out. Sheriff Pilkins said you wouldn't tell him."

"I haven't said I'd accept it," Grandfather said.

"You can use it as an educational fund for Johnny," Willie said.

"The last thing I ever expected to have is an educated grandson," Grandfather said. "But we'll see. As for figuring it out, I'm not proud of that because it took me so long. Seems the professor decided to do some stock market speculating and he got a market tip from someone. He took it to Krohl, and Krohl told him it was no good. The professor insisted, so Krohl accepted the order, which was his job. Then the professor made a bad mistake. Instead of waiting for a statement, and paying for the stock by check, he turned over to Krohl a check he'd just received for the sale of some property in the Upper Peninsula. That endorsed check was the same as cash, and the temptation was too much for Krohl. He had a hot market tip of his own that he thought *was* good, so he faked an account statement showing the purchase of the professor's stock, and he used the money to buy stock for himself."

"He said he was going to wait until the professor's stock went down, and then return all of his money," Willie said. "In that case the professor would have thought he was a hero."

"I know," Grandfather said. "I talked to Hocking this morning, and he told me what was in the confession. The professor never suspected anything because the brokers held his stock certificates for him. All Krohl had to do was to show the purchase on the phony account statement, and make up a certificate number. But then Krohl's troubles started. The professor's tip was a good one, and Krohl's wasn't. The stock he pretended to buy went up—and went up a lot. The stock he did buy went down. By the time he talked the professor into selling the non-existent stock, and did sell the stock he'd bought, there was an eighteen thousand dollar difference between the amount the professor's account statements showed and the actual cash Krohl had on hand.

"The only way out was to talk the professor into buying a stock that would go down, but he found it wasn't easy to pick one. He'd spent his whole business career trying to find stocks that would go up. Finally he managed another fake purchase for the professor, and it turned out to be another mistake. That stock went up, too, though not as much. Then it started down, and he knew if he could talk the professor into holding on long enough to run up a paper loss, he could wipe out the deficit. That was when the professor signed his death certificate. Not only did he insist on selling, but he wanted the money out of the stock, for some speculating in real estate. Krohl came to see him that Tuesday to make a last attempt to get him to hold the stock. When he wouldn't Krohl arranged the experiment in the maze and tried to solve his problem that way. With the professor dead there wasn't anyone to tell him to sell the stock, and though he went through the motions of being concerned about it going down, he didn't actually do anything about it until it went down far enough to clear him. Then he submitted a final phony statement, put the money in the professor's brokerage account, and bragged about how much money he'd saved the estate. The books balanced, and no one suspected him because he didn't know anything about the maze."

"I guess we understand that now," Vaughan said. "But you didn't answer the question. How did you figure it out?"

"I looked through the account statements. All except the last ones had been prepared with an electric typewriter, or some kind of electronic gadget. The type looked just like printing. But the last ones were got out on an ordinary typewriter. This seemed odd, because while it isn't unusual for a company to start using more modern equipment, it shouldn't be happening the other way around. So I bought some stock myself, and when I got my statement it was done by the same gadget that did the professor's old statements. The next step was to compare the letter Krohl had sent me with those typewritten account statements, and they looked as if they were done on the same typewriter. From there it was no trouble getting Hansen to call the Detroit office of Strobel, Ross, Beal and Larkins for a list of the stocks the professor had bought in the last few months. Naturally those purchases Krohl faked weren't on the list, and we knew we had him. You know what happened then."

"I guess we do," Vaughan said. "I also know you led all of us on a merry chase this last week—Willie and I, and the sheriff, and the County Attorney, too. But I suppose as long as you were doing the work you were entitled to get some fun out of it. How did you set the trap?"

"You set part of it yourself, telling Krohl that Pete had to leave town and you were without a caretaker. Then I telephoned him and asked him to meet me at the Courthouse the next morning to go over the professor's brokerage account. He decided there'd have to be a fire that night, to get rid of the account statements."

Vaughan handed over the check. "You certainly earned the money. I hope you come to Wiston College, Johnny, and major in history."

"I wouldn't feel safe studying anything but psychology," I said.

"Don't ask him to explain that," Willie said. "We have a serpent in our midst."

"Just the same, I'm sorry you broke your engagement," I said.

"Think nothing of it, Johnny," Vaughan said. "That's only the third time today that she's given the ring back. She'll probably do it a dozen more times before we're married. But we'll get our license this afternoon and get married on the Fourth of July, and Willie will transfer to Wiston College for her last year. I'll guarantee it. And we'll live happily ever after in the Courthouse, where naturally both of you will always be welcome."

Grandfather chuckled. "Happily ever after? I could tell you a thing or two about that, but I wouldn't want to take all the fun out of your finding it out for yourselves. Willie, Johnny's mother has a Bride's Box in the kitchen. Why don't you ask her for it."

"What on earth is that?" Willie asked.

"It's a recipe box, with all of her favorite recipes. She copies them out as she has time, and then when a bride claims it she gets herself a new box and starts over. Right now it's full. There weren't enough June brides to go around this year, and her box didn't get claimed. Ask her for it."

"This is just your excuse to get me out of the room," Willie said.

Grandfather arched his eyebrows.

"But don't think I don't appreciate it," she went on. "Since Mark is an orphan, I've been hoping that an older man would have a talk with him before our wedding."

She headed for the kitchen, and Grandfather shook his head and said, "She's a terror. I hope you're going into this with your eyes open."

Vaughan grinned. "Wide open."

"There's just one thing that still bothers me. You know, don't you, that it was virtually impossible for a stranger to wander through the maze and happen onto the professor's body."

"The sheriff said the odds were a thousand to one against it," Vaughan said.

"Or ten thousand to one," Grandfather said. "But that's just another way of calling it impossible. Since you did find the body, there's only one possible explanation. You followed Krohl's marks."

"Right. The closer he got to the highway, the more careless he became about erasing them. That's understandable, of course—he was in a panic to get out of there. The first ones I saw looked as if someone had been dragging something. So I followed them. They seemed as good a choice as any, and probably better, because I knew that someone had gone that way."

Grandfather nodded. "And then on the way out you were in something of a panic yourself, and kept losing them."

"Right. But don't mention this to Willie. She hasn't thought of it, and if you don't mind, I'd prefer to have her think that I found the professor on my own initiative."

"Your secret is safe with us," Grandfather said solemnly.

Willie came back with the Bride's Box and we went out on the porch to see them off.

"That Mr. Vaughan isn't such a bad psychologist himself," I told Grandfather.

Grandfather shook his head. "I wouldn't make any bets if I were you. Willie hasn't thought of it, he says. The first spat they have after they're married, she'll tell him all about it. I wonder of Strobel, Ross, Beal and Larkins has appointed a new manager to take Krohl's place."

"Why?" I asked.

"I have ten shares of stock to sell. I haven't received the certificate yet, but that shouldn't keep me from selling."

"Has the stock gone up?"

"I think it's gone down a little."

"Then you'll lose money if you sell."

"I suppose so," Grandfather said. "But I can always charge the loss to that educational fund of yours. I'll telephone now, and then I think I'll go into town and borrow Snubb's paper. I haven't seen a paper for so long that I'm completely out of touch with what's going on in the world. I wonder what kind of a mess our foreign policy has gotten itself into the last week."

"Probably a big one," I said.

"It wouldn't surprise me in the least. You know, Johnny, there's another advantage to living in a small town."

"You mean—nothing ever happens here?"

"You know better than that. But things that happen here are the kind of things a man can understand."

www.ingramcontent.com/pod-product-compliance
Lightning Source LLC
Chambersburg PA
CBHW031129210626
46816CB00015B/1241